rounders

a screenplay by david levien
and brian koppelman

rounders

HYPERION
MIRAMAX
BOOKS

new york

Library of Congress Cataloging-In-Publication Data

Levien, David.
    Rounders : a screenplay / David Levien and Brian Koppelman.
     p. cm.
    ISBN 0-7868-8422-3
    I. Rounders (Motion picture : 1998) II. Koppelman, Brian.
  III. Title.
  PN1997.R679 1998
  791.43′72—dc21   98–30430
                                               CIP

Book Design by Kathy Kikkert

FIRST EDITION

10 9 8 7 6 5 4 3 2 1

rounders

fade in:

Black screen, and a young but wise voice is heard.

(v.o.) mike

Listen, this is the thing: "If you can't spot the sucker in your first half hour at the table, then *you* are the sucker."

int. apartment—night

The place is sparsely decorated with IKEA furniture. A man, MICHAEL McDERMOTT, moves around the place shirtless, and is only seen at angles.

He opens a dresser drawer, takes out a turtleneck, and puts it on.

He moves to the closet. On the shelf are several baseball caps that advertise seed companies, trucks, sports teams. Mike's hand moves along the row and selects a beat-up REO Speedwagon cap. He puts it on. Beneath the cap are two paper-clipped packets of five thousand dollars each. Mike pockets them.

Mike fishes in the pocket of a Foxwood's jacket and pulls out two more five-thousand-dollar packets.

He puts on a leather jacket, then turns to the dresser and picks up a pack of cigarettes. He puts them in his pocket but leaves a cigarette lighter sitting there.

Walking through the apartment toward the door, Mike passes a bookshelf.

ANGLE ON: The bookshelf is split into two distinct groupings. One shelf contains the standard first- and second-year law-school casebooks. The other holds the requisite readings on poker: Yardley; King; Alvarez; Caro's Book of Tells; Slansky's Theory of Poker; and the bible, the silver-covered opus, The Super System by Doyle Brunson.

Mike takes The Super System off the shelf, opens it and withdraws two more packets of five thousand dollars each. He pockets them as well and heads out the door.

ext. street—night

Mike walks alone, hands stuffed into coat pockets, head down, along a dark New York street. He is obscured by a wall of steam that jets up from a manhole.

(v.o.) mike

Guys around here'll tell you, you play for a living, it's like any
other job. You don't gamble, you grind it out. Your goal is to win
one big bet an hour. That's it. Get your money in when you have
the best of it, protect it when you don't. Don't give anything away.

He turns down an alley.

ext. building—same

He reaches the door to a broken-down building and enters.

int. cage elevator—same

*Mike rides in the cramped and ancient elevator. Seen in the dim light, he is
almost thirty, slim, the baseball cap pulled all the way down to his brow,
turtleneck hiked all the way up to his chin. The bit of face showing in between
is pasty white and expressionless.*

(v.o.) mike

So they say, and yes I did. One year, seven months, thirteen days.
A true grinder. Managed to play my way through the first three
semesters of law school and build a bankroll day by day, dollar by
dollar, bet by bet.

*The elevator stops and Mike pulls its rusty accordion door open. He stares at
another door, a forbidding orange metal one with no handle.*

*An eye slat slides back and a round face is visible on the other side. The face
chews.*

*He is TEDDY KGB, a burly Russian in his early fifties. With his thicket of black
curly hair, he bears an uncomfortable resemblance to Vasily Alexiev.*

*KGB fits an Oreo into his mouth and with a throwing of bolts and tumblers
lets Mike in.*

int. KGB's card room—same

The faint, ever-present riffle of clay checks can be heard.

*A bare Manhattan card room. Fluorescent tubes, once-white walls, and green
felt card tables. A television shows the Yankees.*

Several players monitor their cards and their red, green, and white checks.

So I learned how to win a little at a time, but finally, I've learned this: If you're too careful, your whole life can become a fucking grind.

Teddy KGB offers Mike an Oreo from his bag before sidling over to a sturdy built-in desk.

teddy kgb

Five hundred?

KGB's accent is heavy eastern European. He moves for a rack of red and green checks.

mike

Not tonight, Teddy.

teddy kgb

No. What?

Mike removes the clipped packets of money from his pockets.

mike

Three stacks of high society.

Teddy sticks an Oreo in his mouth and chews slowly. He looks at Mike's roll and his hand moves to a rack of black and gold checks. He puts stacks in front of Mike.

teddy kgb

Thirty thousand. Count it.

Mike tosses his wad as casually as he can on the desk. He counts the chips by stack height, then puts them back into their racks.

mike

It's right.

teddy kgb

So, you're sitting the apple. Good. Want a cookie?

mike

No.

Just then a man walks out of the bathroom. He is JOEY KNISH. Knish is fencing with forty, tall and gaunt, wearing gray gym sweats and smooth Foster Grants. Knish walks towards Mike.

(v.o.) mike
Joey Knish is a New York legend. He's been a rounder, earning his living at cards, since he was fifteen years old. Knish says if there's a degenerate who's on the scene in New York the past twenty years, he's either sat with him, bet with him, taken him, or been taken by him. So far as I know this is the truth. He's as close to a friend as there is in this place, but today I don't want to see him.

Knish takes note of the racks Mike holds.

knish
What're you, holding those for someone?

mike
Yeah, I'm holding 'em for you.

knish
You should be, 'cause I hope you're not thinking of putting all that glimmer in play.

Mike shrugs. Knish looks around and motions Mike to a corner. He speaks quietly now.

knish
You don't wanna butt onions with these guys. They'll chew you up. Take your whole bankroll.

Knish points at Mike's checks.

mike
So you say.

knish
Plenty of easy games. We get outta here, get some coffee, ride over to that soft seat in Queens.

mike
I'm sitting with the top guys tonight.

knish

You're not ready.

mike

Fuck you.

knish

What I'm telling you is, I'm not the one's gonna get fucked you sit no-limit. Watch 'em from two tables away, fine. Stand on the rail, great. But don't sit down with 'em, you can only lose.

Mike puts a cigarette in his mouth, but leaves it unlit.

knish

Why're you doing this?

Mike says nothing.

knish

KGB didn't get that house up in Pound Ridge losing to part-time players like you.

mike

I know what I'm doing.

Knish pauses.

knish

You're making a run at it, aren't you? Rolling up a stake and going to Vegas. I'm right, right?

mike

I can beat the game.

knish

Look, maybe this is a game can be beat, but you *know* you can beat the ten-twenty at the Chesterfield, and the Hi-Lo at that goulash joint on Seventy-ninth Street.

Mike just stares at him.

knish

Okay. I unnerstand, I unnerstand. . . . Back to battle, then.

Knish walks off and rejoins one of the games in progress. Mike moves through the club toward the back room.

int. back card room—later

(v.o.) mike
The game in question is no-limit Texas Hold 'Em. Minimum buy-in twenty-five thousand dollars. A game like this doesn't come together often outside the casinos. The stakes attract rich flounders, and they in turn attract the sharks. There are pros in from three states for this one.

A small room dominated by a card table is crammed with the bodies of players. There are a few railbirds tucked in the corners, and a few SIZEABLE RUSSIAN SPECTATORS. There is hardly room to move a chair back without hitting the wall.

There is the constant sound of clattering checks, decks being made, and chatter. A thick cloud of cigarette smoke hovers above the action.

NOTE: Unless otherwise mentioned, every cardplayer sports at least one ring on each hand, usually a twinkling diamond or gold-and-onyx number, and most often worn on the pinky.

Mike, Teddy KGB, and eight other serious guys huddle around the table. Mike is the youngest by ten years and fifty pounds. He sits with an unlit cigarette hanging from his lip.

The game is always self-dealt. On this hand SY deals. SY—sixty-five years old, bald but for a crown of fringe, corduroy jacket, Sans-a-belt slacks.

ZAGOSH is fifty with bad dentures and a Members Only wardrobe.

zagosh
Blinds up.

First two guys to Sy's left put in their checks.

(v.o.) mike
No-limit Texas Hold 'Em is the Cadillac of poker. Each player is dealt two cards face down. Five cards are then dealt face up across the middle. The first three are called the flop. The next one is

called the turn. The final card is known as the river. These are community cards that everyone can use.

All the board cards are dealt and discreetly looked over. A few bets go in, a few hands are folded.

The action goes around to IRVING. Tremendous in size and dressed in white shirt, black coat, yarmulke, beard. He puts eight black chips in.

irving

Raise, an eight ball.

The next two guys, TONY and FALOOB watch, having folded previously.

Mike throws in his cards.

mike

South Street.

Zagosh does the same.

zagosh

Ouch.

Kenny—linebacker's build twenty long years ago—acts. He puts in checks.

kenny

Call, Irv. Take a suck on these babies—the Brass Brazilians.

Kenny turns over a pair of aces.

irving

Fucking spikes crush my ladies.

Irving sends his queens into the muck, gets up to leave.

kenny

You know, truth be told, Irving, I'm surprised to see a guy like you in here the first place.

SAVINO—crisply dressed and coiffed, Paul Anka style.

savino

That's the thing with the skullcaps, the big con. Everyone thinks they're beyond reproach, but some of the biggest fucking degenerates I know wear 'em.

irving

Don't talk that way about my fucking people.

savino

Your "people." Please, Irv, you're the only Jew I know took Germany plus the points.

Irving waves him off and leaves. Kenny collects his pot, and Sy rakes in the cards to clean the deck for an upcoming deal, but takes a few of Kenny's checks with him. Several at the table notice. There is a PAUSE. . . .

Sy "innocently" stacks the checks with his own.

savino (to himself)

Fucking cocksucker. (ALOUD) Teddy, this fucking cocksucker, what's your name?—Sy—just fucking kited the pot.

All action at the table stops dead.

(v.o.) mike

The first thing you do when there's a disturbance at the table is cover your chips and watch the cards.

sy

Who?

savino

You. I saw you rake the chips in and put 'em in your stack.

sy

No, no. Those? A few, by accident. I, uh, was about to give 'em to Kenny.

savino

I waited to see. Once you stacked 'em, you stole 'em.

Everyone at the table pipes up in anger now. Sy turns to Mike to back his appeal.

sy

You know me, you've seen me around, I wouldn't—

Mike slides his chair away from Sy like he's rotten meat.

mike

I don't know this guy, I'm not with 'im.

teddy kgb (to sy)

Get outta here.

Sy gets ready to protest.

teddy kgb

No. I saw it.

Resigned, Sy starts to collect his checks.

teddy kgb

Leave it.

sy

What?

teddy kgb

I said fucking go.

Sy is escorted out by the few SIZEABLE RUSSIAN SPECTATORS.

(v.o.) mike

All the soft places in New York this guy could have picked for check copping, and he had to try Teddy KGB's. For a few hundred a hand he loses his whole buy-in, and believe me, that's not all he loses.

ANGLE ON: Mike sees Sy dragged into the cage elevator. As the door is sliding closed, the first blows are already landing on Sy. A knee to the gut. A chopping left to the head. The door closes all the way.

Teddy pays Kenny his stolen checks from Sy's stack. A LARGE RUSSIAN swings by and collects the rest of the stack.

Another RUSSIAN removes the empty chair and the players' bodies automatically shift and fill the space.

savino

You believe this fucking guy, walkin' in here?

teddy kgb

Okay, let's play some cards.

The next hand is dealt and Mike looks back to his hand.

int. back card room—much later

Things have condensed, there are only three players left besides Mike—Teddy, Savino, and an Asian guy named HENRY LIN. Lin is forty, wire-rimmed glasses, baseball hat.

Teddy and Henry Lin are in charge of the table based on their large stacks. Mike is doing well with fifty thousand dollars in front of him.

(v.o.) mike

No-Limit. There's no other game in which fortunes can change so much from hand to hand. A brilliant player can get a strong hand cracked, go "on tilt" and lose his mind along with every single chip in front of him. This is why the World Series of poker is decided over a no-limit Hold 'Em table. Some people, pros even, won't play No-Limit. They can't handle the swings.

Mike deals. Blinds go up. The first two cards go out.

(v.o.) mike

But there are others, like Doyle Brunson, who consider No-Limit the only pure game left. I guess I feel the same way. Like Papa Wallenda said, "Life is on the wire, the rest is just waiting."

Angle on Mike's cards—A–C, 9–C.

lin

Fold.

mike

I gotta raise. Five hundred.

                    teddy kgb

'S a position raise. I call it.

                     savino

Pasadena.

He folds. Knish walks into the room and watches.

The flop comes—A–S, 9–S, 8–C.

                    teddy kgb

Go 'head.

                   (v.o.) mike

Here's the beauty of this game. I flop top two, and I wanna keep
him in the hand. Against your average guy I'd set a bear
trap—hardly bet at all, let him walk into it. But KGB's too smart
for that. So what I've gotta do is overbet the pot—make it look like
I'm trying to buy it. Then he plays back at me, and I get paid off.

Mike puts in chips.

                      mike

Two thousand, Teddy. The bet's two thousand dollars.

*Teddy looks at Mike, puts an Oreo in his mouth and slowly chews. Then he
acts.*

                    teddy kgb

I call.

                   (v.o.) mike

I put Teddy on a flush draw.

                    teddy kgb

Burn and turn.

The card comes, 9–H. Mike's hand is nines full of aces.

                    teddy kgb

To the bettor . . .

                       11

                              mike
Check's good.

                          (v.o.) mike
Now I hope a spade falls and Teddy makes his flush. That way
he'll bet strong and I'll beat him with my full house.

The river card comes, Q–S.

                           teddy kgb
I'm gonna bet. Bet, fifteen thousand.

                              mike
Time.

*Mike pauses as if he's deciding whether to call. He seems anguished over
whether or not he should bet.*

                          (v.o.) mike
I want him to think that I'm pondering a call, but all I'm really
thinking about is Vegas and the fucking Mirage.

mike

I don't think you've got spades. I'm gonna raise, Teddy.

Mike counts his stacks and pushes all his remaining checks into the pot.

mike

All in. Thirty-three thousand.

Teddy's reaction is immediate, he pushes stacks of checks in.

teddy kgb

You're right, I don't have spades—

(v.o.) mike

I know before the cards are even turned over.

Teddy shows his hand.

teddy kgb

Aces full, Mike.

Mike sits there looking stunned, as if he just took a shovel blow to the face.

Teddy KGB smiles once briefly, his teeth black with Oreo, then rakes in the pot and the game breaks up. After a swing like this, it's over.

Mike is immobile. He now sits alone.

Knish comes up behind him with a conciliatory pat on the shoulder.

> **knish**
> C'mon, get up. Walk it off.

> **mike**
> I can't move.

> **knish**
> We'll talk about it. I'll buy you breakfast. Then we can go over to the Tenth Street Baths and have a schvitz.

> **mike**
> I couldn't even afford the steam.

ext. street—day

Mike is slumped against the side of the building. Knish lights up a joint and talks through a lungful of smoke.

> **knish**
> Tapped. Didn't leave yourself any outs.

> **mike**
> I'm down to the felt, Knish. Lost my whole bankroll. My case money and my tuition, too.

Knish proffers the bone. Mike shakes it off.

> **knish**
> Happens to everyone. Time to time everyone goes bust. You'll be back in the game before you know it.

> **mike**
> I'm done, Joey. I'm out of it.

knish

They all say at first. . . . Anyway, let me stake ya. Standard deal, fifty percent of your winnings. You lose, it's on me.

Mike looks at Knish.

mike

I'd just throw it away. . . . You still got the truck?

tableau—nine months later

ext. kappock street, yonkers—night

A dingy ten-ton GMC truck rumbles down the road.

int. truck cab—same

Mike drives the truck, pulling on a cup of road coffee between gears.

He looks tired in a way he didn't at the poker table, and he might've put on just a few pounds.

(v.o.) mike

You don't hear much about guys who take their shot and miss. But *I'll* tell you what happens to 'em—they end up humping crappy jobs, on graveyard shifts, trying to figure how they came up short.

The truck pulls over.

(v.o.) mike

Knish originally got this bakery truck during a run of cold cards. Now he leases it out to rounders looking for steady money. I'm the fourth guy the past five years to bust out, give up the game, and drive this route.

ext. stop n' sip—same

Mike slides out of the cab and opens the back.

(v.o.) mike

At least the fourth guy to break the cardinal fucking rule: Always leave yourself outs. Applies to a player's life away from the game same as it does at the table.

He loads a hand truck with cases of Pepsi and Little Debbies snacks.

int. stop n' sip—same

The store's tiny interior is crammed with low-cost goods and food. A lone hot dog sweats on spinning silver rollers. Mike wheels in the goods.

Behind the counter a gaunt, unshaven man, MOOGIE, leans and reads the paper. He gestures where Mike should put the stuff.

Mike steps to the counter for Moogie's signature on the slip.

> **moogie**
> Lemme ask you somethin'. In a legal sense, can fucking Steinbrenner really move the Yankees? Does he have the fucking right to just move 'em?

Moogie signs the slip and Mike takes it back.

> **mike**
> How do I know?

> **moogie**
> You din't learn that yet?

> **mike**
> No. I think they teach about Steinbrenner the third year of law school.

Moogie shrugs and Mike wheels the hand truck out.

ext. city law university—night

Establishing shot of the law school near Lincoln Center.

int. dean petrovsky's office—very late

A wood-paneled lawyer's office that would look a lot more decorous if six men, mostly in their sixties, weren't sitting around a hastily cleared desk playing cards. Their game is Ten-twenty-dollar Seven-Stud.

A light knock is heard and the door swings open. Mike enters.

(v.o.) mike
The judges' game. I'd heard about it for years on the street, before I was even in law school. A rotating group of ten or twelve judges, prosecutors, and professors. They all have money, and in my playing days it would have been pretty sweet to have any of them owing me favors. Only problem is, no one can get in the game anymore. One rounder, Crispy Linetta, sat under some pretense, but when they found out he was a pro, he couldn't cross the street without a legal hassle. Even his regular club, Vorshay's, got shut down. Place'd been open since 1907.

DEAN ABE PETROVSKY, a large, bearded man, presides over the game. He waves Mike in. He speaks with a Brooklyn/Israeli accent.

petrovsky
Michael, you've got some things for me?

JUDGE EUGENE MARINACCI—New York State Supreme Court, has coloring to match his cigar ash.

judge marinacci
Kid, he paying you for this late-night shit?

mike
Knowledge is my only reward, sir.

judge marinacci
Let me tell ya, it ain't worth it. Why'nt ya become a jockey. Do something useful.

JUDGE KAPLAN, Court of Appeals, prunish-looking.

judge kaplan
Kid's a little tall, isn't he, Gene?

D.A. SHIELDS, a bald, hard-looking guy with a deep South Shore accent.

d.a. shields

Enough with the Belmont recruiting spiel, bet's to you, Kappy.

petrovsky

Michael is heading the defense in the moot court you're presiding over next week, Gene. Besides, he needs the background if he's going to clerk for one of you this summer.

A groan goes up from the table. EISEN, a big-voiced, gray, older guy.

eisen

Abe, I thought ya liked the kid, why ya want to make him a civil servant?

D.A. Shields leans over conspiratorily.

d.a. shields

Word to the wise: Stay in the private sector. That Nassau defense attorney's game—they use our chips for coasters.

Their game continues. PROFESSOR GREEN, very much the academic type, is first to fold.

Mike removes files from his bag and puts them in the corner of the office.

d.a. shields

Call.

eisen

Call.

(v.o.) mike

The amazing thing is, in this collection of great legal minds, there isn't a single real cardplayer.

Mike creeps up behind Petrovsky as the bet comes to him. Before Abe can act, Mike impulsively pushes in a portion of his chips.

mike

Raise. The professor raises.

Mike receives some serious ruffled stares. He wears a broad smile on his face, though.

(v.o.) mike

I don't know if I'm going to bring my legal career to a crashing
halt before it even starts, but I just can't help myself.

petrovsky (whispers to mike)

You're sure, Michael? I would have probably just called.

mike

You're good.

petrovsky

Okay, raise it is.

The players grudgingly call the bet. The final card comes for each, face down.

judge marinacci

Check.

judge kaplan

Check to Martin and Lewis over there.

d.a. shields

Check to the raiser.

eisen

Czechoslovakia.

Abe goes to show Mike his last card, which Mike hardly glances at.

mike

What's the limit?

judge marinacci

Twenty dollars. The big bet's twenty dollars.

mike

Good. Twenty-dollar bet for the professor.

d.a. shields

You've seen half the hand, how the fuck're you betting into us?

judge kaplan

Always the prosecutor, eh, Barry?

eisen

You sure this is wise, Abe? It's your money the kid's betting with.

mike

It's plenty wise, because we know what we're holding, and we *know* what you're holding.

judge marinacci

The fuck you know what we all have.

mike

A summer clerkship in your office says I do.

judge marinacci

I don't bet with jobs like that, but let's just say I'll put you at the top of the list if you're right.

mike

Okay. You were looking for that third three, but you forgot that Professor Green folded it on Fourth Street and you're doing your best to represent that you have it. The D.A. made his two pair, but he knows they're no good here. Judge Kaplan was looking to squeeze out that diamond flush, but he came up short. And Mr. Eisen is futilely hoping that his queens'll stand up. Like I said, the professor's bet is twenny dollars.

Looks range from amazement to disgust as cards are thrown into the muck. Petrovsky rakes in his unexpected pot.

eisen

eisen

What'd you have, Abe?

petrovsky

Nothing but a busted straight.

Howls of indignance from the assembled crew go up.

judge marinacci

All right, kid, your first assignment—pull up a seat next to me.

Mike picks up his bag.

mike

I'd like to, Judge . . . but I don't play cards.

Mike exits.

judge marinacci

I like the kid, Abe. . . .

The game continues.

int. truck—later

Mike drives the truck and looks miserable doing so.

(v.o.) mike

I tell ya, it was hard leaving that game. An open invitation to lay with those lambs—but I'm retired. The truth is I can always find games, though. Easy games, tough games, straight games, crooked games, home games. I could turn this truck south onto the Jersey Turnpike and be at the Taj in two hours. Instead I'm heading north into nowhere, delivering baked goods.

ext. warehouse—day

Mike locks up the truck and pulls down a steel door behind it before going on his way.

ext. apartment building—later

Mike enters his five-story walk-up.

int. apartment—same

He tosses his keys on the table and sits down. JO, his significant other, walks out of the bedroom.

She is minimalist, beautiful, and a bit tightly wound. Not a woman who'd take kindly to the suggestion she dress it up and show it off a little. She wears a professional pantsuit and is ready to leave for her day.

> **jo**
>
> How'd it go?

> **mike**
>
> Sick of that fucking route.

> **jo**
>
> You're almost done with it. Few more semesters, your name'll be on some firm's letterhead.

> **mike**
>
> Yeah.

> **jo**
>
> Don't sound so excited. . . . Anyway, I'm already late for work.

She leans down and gives him a peck. He pulls her down onto his lap, looking for more.

> **jo**
>
> Come on, Mike. Don't tempt me.

He begins kissing at her neck and ear.

> **mike**
>
> Tempt *you*? Could hardly keep the truck on the road thinking 'bout you here all alone last night.

He persists.

> **jo**
>
> Mike, please.

mike

C'mon, you know you can't resist.

Jo is kissing him back. They're all over each other.

jo

I don't have time, baby.

mike

I'll be quick. You won't even feel a thing.

jo

We both know that's not true.

Jo pulls herself free, gets up, straightens her outfit.

Mike goes to the kitchen sink and splashes water on his face.

mike

I'm telling you, Jo, these long nights are killing me.

jo

They never used to.

mike

Those nights didn't seem long. Buy in at eight, look up and it's morning. Next thing you know, it's dark again.

jo

Well, at least the semester's almost over.

Mike hesitates for a moment.

mike

Yeah, and you know what? I think I'm all set for the summer.

jo

What do you mean?

mike

After I left you at the library, I impressed Judge Marinacci. Looks like I'm in line for a clerkship.

She eyes him, waiting for an explanation.

mike

Hear me out, now. The judges were playing cards, and I read Marinacci's hand blind.

Jo stiffens.

jo

So instead of coming home, you played cards with some judge?

mike

No, no. I wasn't even playing. I just caught his eye by seeing through their cards. Now, as long as I don't fuck up moot court, the job'll be mine.

jo

That's terrific, Michael. Really. A fucking parlor trick. You'll be a great help to him when he writes an opinion on high-stakes poker.

She gathers her briefcase.

mike

C'mon, babe, you're the one who told me I should bring my poker skills to the courtroom.

jo

Please. What I meant was you should use your head. The way you read people, the way you can calculate odds on the spot. I didn't mean you should con your way into a summer job.

She grabs her bag and heads for door.

mike

Con? I was networking.

Jo stops and speaks patiently.

jo

You don't get it. You'll be no different than those ex-college athletes—secure job with the D.A.'s office, as long as they never miss a Lawyers' League game. If you get in this way, Mike, you'll always be a hustler to them.

mike

Yeah? But I didn't even sit with them, Jo. I didn't play.

Jo puts on her coat and walks out.

ext. hall—same

Mike calls down the steps to her.

mike

Hate to ask, but can I take the Jeep tomorrow?

jo

Where?

mike

Worm's getting out, gotta pick him up.

jo

Tomorrow, beautiful.

mike

I promised I'd be there.

jo

Worm . . . I can't even believe you still know someone called Worm.

mike

The guy's like my brother, Jo.

She continues down the stairs.

mike

Shit, didn't even play.

int. dayroom—day

A pale gray-painted dayroom in Baldinger State Correctional Facility, Dannemora, New York. Bare tables and chairs are the room's only furniture.

A game of hearts is taking place between a few inmates. Most of them have long hair, and are large and imposing in their jumpsuits, even if they do have shower sandals on their feet.

One guy, the smallest by a foot and wearing a patchy handlebar mustache, is LES MURPHY—also known as WORM.

One of his opponents is ROY, and Roy is not happy.

roy
Motherfucker, that's the fourth time you've laid the bitch of spades on me.

worm
Is it? No, hand before last I was stuck with Black Maria.

roy
Yeah, but you shot the moon on that hand, so it helped you.

worm
I'm just saying, you didn't get it four times. Anyhow, that's five hundred, I think. So . . . we're done here.

Worm gathers up several packs of cigarettes from each of the players. One of the losers, DERALD, is sore.

derald
You ain't walking outta here wit our 'grits, Worm.

worm

The fuck do you mean? I'll hold 'em like always, I won't smoke 'em. You get double or nothing tomorrow.

A buzzer sounds and a crew-cut GUARD enters the room.

guard

Murphy! The hell are you sitting here for? You're processed. Come on.

roy

Processed? This motherfucker's getting the jump?

Worm tries to look surprised.

derald

Man, have some decency. You can buy all the smokes you want in half an hour. . . :

worm

What're you talking about? I won these.

derald

You don't even smoke, Worm. . . .

worm

All right, all right. Here you go.

Worm takes an open pack from his jumpsuit pocket and shakes a few loose ones out onto the table.

roy

Ain't a good idea to add insult to injury. That shit'll come back on ya.

worm

Yeah? Not in this lifetime, Homes. Enjoy your time.

Worm saunters out.

ext. prison gate—later

Across the street from the gray, menacing prison, Mike leans against a Jeep Cherokee.

(v.o.) mike
I met Worm at Dwight Englewood Preparatory Academy over in Jersey. We were the only two scumbags attending. My father's office was there. It said "Custodian" on the door. That's why they took me. Worm's dad did the grounds, when he wasn't too fucking drunk—that's when we did 'em. . . . Of course the grounds weren't all we did. Worm put us into a scam a day on all the young aristocrats we went to school with. Selling dime bags of oregano, nunchakus, and fire crackers from Chinatown. Kept us in lunch money.

int. prison property room—same

Worm stands in a storage-type room that has boxes of belongings behind a chain-link fence.

(v.o.) mike
One time we got the starting five to take a dive against Long Island Friends. Worm got tossed out over that one. The fucking point guard cracked. Worm didn't, though. I would've been right out with him if he had.

A GUARD passes Worm a box that holds his street clothes. Upon receipt of them Worm notices that something seems to be missing. Worm digs around in the box and discovers a toothpick. He nods, pops it in his mouth, and seems very satisfied.

ext. prison gate—later

Worm is let out of the prison gate. He walks toward Mike, now wearing street clothes—black pants and a black leather sport coat like Shaft's.

(v.o.) mike
Since he's been away I feel like I've been marking time, serving a sentence right along with 'im.

The moment Mike and Worm see each other the air is full of many things: joy, relief, memories, a bittersweet sadness.

They embrace.

> **worm**
> Mike. I knew you'd be here, man. Never let me down, never.

> **mike**
> Would've been here every month if you—

> **worm**
> Nah. Didn't want you to see me like that.

> **mike**
> Great to see you now, Corporal. . . . It wasn't the same with you gone. They toughen you up any inside?

Mike puts Worm in a friendly headlock.

> **worm**
> Nice car. Looks like you're prospering.

> **mike**
> I borrowed it.

Worm discards his toothpick.

worm

Then get in your borrowed car and drive us far the fuck away from this place.

int. jeep—later

Mike drives, Worm rides and smokes.

worm

. . . So I got three games going on a regular basis. One with the *shvatzorum,* one with the *gringos,* and one with the hacks. And the trick is, I gotta make enough cash in the white game to lose in the hack game. And I gotta trim enough smokes from the brothers to keep myself in the style to which I've become accustomed, without getting the shit kicked outta me.

mike

Tools?

Worm raises his hands.

mike

Ah, *solo las manos.*

worm

Painting's outta the question. Only an asshole'd be holding evidence inside. Wait'll you see whatta artist I've become.

Mike laughs.

worm

You?

mike

Forget about it. I don't mess with the railroad bible anymore.

worm

You're shitting me.

mike

I got cleaned out.

worm
Mikey McDee? I don't believe it.

mike
Yeah, it was a real blood game over at KGB's place.

worm
Mad Russian emptied your pockets?

mike
Didn't want to tell you while you were in there—dispirit you like that.

Worm plays with the radio, finds a song.

worm
So it's just law school now, huh? What about money?

mike
I'm driving Knish's truck.

worm
Jesus. Well, don't you worry, son. The cavalry is here—

mike
Don't even think about it. I'm not playing. I'm done.

worm
Sure you're done. Just like you were done flipping baseball cards in junior high after you lost 'em all. Like you were done with women when Chrissy Rapoza left you blue balled that whole weekend down the shore . . . Now, listen, I know a game—a real berry patch just outside the city.

Mike gives Worm a glance.

mike
Well, I'll drop you.

ext. princeton university campus—evening

The Jeep drives past idyllic ivy-covered buildings.

ext. waterton lodge—same

They park in front of a building that looks like a fraternity house that would be listed in the Robb Report.

(v.o.) mike
Waterton Lodge is an eating club at Princeton University. One of those clubs that has been around for generations, where the sons of the well-heeled dine and socialize. This one is invitation only, and the chances that guys like us would rate one are about the same as making a double belly-buster straight draw. Leave it to the Worm—not only does he know about the backroom card game, but manages to burrow himself in, too.

They get out of the car.

worm
I know a girl named Barbara. She's fucking hot. I was this close to banging her before I went away. She's the hostess here. I walk in, I'm her "cousin" from outta town, new to poker . . .

Mike nods.

mike
Sounds solid. Nice hookup.

worm
Pretty damn nice, only one problem. I got this feeling?

mike
Which feeling's that exactly?

worm
You know the feeling. You got your table all set . . .

mike
Yeah.

worm
You got your knife and fork . . .

mike
Uh-huh.

worm

You got your sauce there, your A-1, your Luger's—

Mike reaches into his pocket and pulls out his money clip.

mike

Only thing missing's the stake.

worm

Exactly. A nickel should get me started.

Mike's face pinches. His roll is looking anemic. After the first hundred he peels, there are only twenties.

worm

Damn, how you livin'?

mike

A little light. I told you. Anyway, I've got two-twenty for you.

worm

Shit, that's only yoleven big bets. Not even enough to establish table image.

mike

Good, so forget this game. I'll straighten you out tomorrow in the city.

worm

Need to get started tonight. I'm already behind.

mike

You just got out, what's the fucking hurry?

worm

The hurry? At least five guys been waiting on my release.

mike

How much you owe?

worm

Over ten. Can't even figure the juice. . . . Two-twenty, damn.

Maybe a *cardplayer* could get something going with two-twenty . . .

Mike looks at Worm, then shakes his head.

mike
I heard you asking in the car, and I hear you now, but I can't do it. I just can't do it. I've made promises.

Worm shrugs.

worm
Okay. I understand. I respect that, and it's all right, and I'll be fine. I'll just have to make some moves early that might play better to a later audience. . . . Not the first time . . .

Mike hands Worm the money.

mike
Premium hands, buddy.

worm
I'll make sure of it. . . .

Worm gives Mike a handshake and heads for the inn.

worm
And Mike?

mike
Yeah?

worm
It's great to see you, man.

Mike turns around and gets in the car.

int. jeep—later

Mike drives grimly, his eyes fixed straight ahead. The radio plays quietly. He doesn't take his eyes off the road.

Mike's face takes on a granite expression. He jerks the wheel to the right and stands on the brake. The Jeep churns gravel on the shoulder of the road.

int. waterton lodge—later

Mike enters the club, which resembles an intimate restaurant. Oil portraits hang on wood-paneled walls, the tables are dark, polished wood. Young diners sit comfortably in hunter green, hundred-year-old leather chairs.

Mike takes out a pack of cigarettes and slips a much-folded hundred-dollar-bill from the lining. He puts a cigarette in his mouth, but doesn't light it.

(v.o.) mike

In his *Confessions of a Winning Poker Player,* Jack King said, "Few players recall big pots they have won—strange as it seems—but every player can remember with remarkable accuracy the outstanding tough beats of his career." Seems true to me, 'cause walking in here I can hardly remember how I built my bankroll, but I can't stop thinking of how I lost it.

At a desk near the door, BARBARA—tall, olive complexion, far too attractive for the Ivy League—takes coats and acts as hostess.

barbara

You must be Mike. . . .

mike

Uh-huh.

barbara

Worm said you'd be joining him.

Mike is poker-faced.

barbara

Come with me.

She leads him through the dining room. Mike's head swivels discreetly at the rich appointment of the room.

mike

I'm not here to play, just keep company.

barbara

No, no, that's no good. See, here's the play, you're my new
boyfriend looking for a regular game.

mike

I'm not much of a cardplayer.

barbara

Bullshit. Worm told me that's precisely what you are. . . . My cut's
twenty-five percent.

mike

I see.

int. den—same

*She leads him into a small, private den, which is even woodier and clubbier
than the outer room.*

*Around a gleaming oak table sit five guys in tweed with elbow patches,
and—incongruously—Worm.*

barbara

Gentlemen, this is my boyfriend, Michael.

A ripple of greetings goes up.

barbara

Be nice to him. Leave him enough to buy me breakfast.

She gives Mike a warm kiss on the lips.

barbara

Good luck, honey.

*Barbara leaves and Mike sits down. As all the guys introduce themselves,
Mike buys chips with his matchstick hundred.*

mike

Deal me in, I guess.

The dealer is Worm.

The game's Chicago.

BIRCH, milk-blond hair, bad skin, reedy voice, speaks to Mike.

birch

You know Chicago?

mike

Remind me.

birch

Stud game, high spade in the hole wins half the pot.

Antes go in, and Worm deals the first three cards to each player.

ANGLE ON MIKE'S CARDS: Next to a J–H, he has the ace of spades in the hole.

Mike gives Worm a look.

int. den—later

Mike is starting to build a large stack of checks while Worm is just holding on. A hand has been dealt out to the river.

wagner

Are you at university, Michael?

birch

Check.

mike

No. I go to law school, in the city. Raise fifty.

higgins

Call. Columbia?

mike

City Law, night.

STEINY, tortoiseshell glasses, curly hair.

steiny

Call. Nights? You must be quite industrious.

Mike smiles affably.

birch

Call.

mike

My pedigree wasn't as spotless as all yours I guess. . . . I'm full.

Mike turns his cards over and rakes in the pot.

As the next hands are dealt, quick cuts show the moves Mike and Worm make.

(v.o.) mike

Worm and I fall into our old rhythm like Clyde Frazier and Pearl Monroe. We bring out all the old school tricks. Stuff that would never play in the city—signaling, chip placing, trapping; we even run the old best hand play. I can probably crack the game just as quickly straight up, but there's no risk in this room. Now, some people might look down on Worm's mechanics, call it immoral, but as Canada Bill Jones said, "It's immoral to let a sucker keep his money." Like they teach you in One-L, *Caveat emptor,* pal.

Mike takes another pot.

(v.o.) mike

Worm really has become an artist, too. Discard Culls, Pickup Culls, Overhand Runups, The Double Duke—his technique is flawless. But his judgment is a little off. A few times I have to fold the case hand just so it won't be obvious. Still, he plays the part of the loser to perfection. . . .

Worm is out of chips. He stands up and puts on his jacket.

worm

Like my uncle Murphy says, "When the last dime is gone, it's time to move on." Thanks a fucking lot guys. I'm outta here.

The guys chortle at his misfortune.

Come back anytime. Your money's always good here. . . .

Worm exits.

int. waterton lodge main room—later

The place is cleaned up and shut down for the night. Barbara is near the door as the guys come through the dining room. The card game is over.

birch
Your boyfriend's lucky in love and lucky in cards. He won every hand there at the end.

steiny
Just the hands he played, Birch. I'm going home, I have an eight o'clock tomorrow.

The players put on coats. Mike slips his arm around Barbara.

mike
Only bad thing about cards is it keeps me away from you, sweetheart.

The players leave. Barbara shuts the lights and she and Mike step outside.

ext. waterton lodge parking lot—same

Mike has his arm around her intimately as they walk to her car. She checks the parking lot to make sure everyone is gone then knocks on the roof of her car. When Mike sees it's clear he steps back from her. Worm pops up and gets out.

worm
Cut up the green.

Mike takes out a wad of cash—mostly fifties and twenties. He counts it and hands Barbara hers.

mike
Yours is three hundred.

barbara

Thank you, boys.

worm

When can we see you again?

barbara

Give it a few—

mike

No, no. I'm done. This one was just, just because.

barbara

All right then, boys.

Barbara gets in her car and drives off. Mike and Worm linger for a moment.

mike

How'd you know I'd come?

worm

Josey Wales, The Preacher, The Man with No Name. Clint always doubles back when a friend's in need.

Mike smiles and flips Worm the keys to the Jeep.

ext. george washington bridge, upper level—morning

The Jeep moves over the Hudson, Manhattan rising ahead of it.

ext. west side parking lot—later

Mike and Worm get out of the Jeep and Mike turns the keys over to an ATTENDANT. Worm reads his watch.

worm

Six fifty-two. We made nice time. Breakfast?

mike

Nah. I have to fucking get home—if she hasn't changed the locks on me. And I barely have time for a shower before my meeting.

worm

Come on, I'll pick the lock for ya. I'm thinking waffles, egg sandwich. I'm buying.

mike

Save your money for once. I can't. I'll see you later.

worm

At least could you straighten me out before you go?

Mike hesitates.

mike

All right, I'll skip the shower. Come on. . . .

They walk toward Seventh Avenue, heading east.

ext. high rise—a bit later

A plush-looking building in the mid-twenties between Park and Madison.

worm

Here? Real carpet joint, huh?

Mike pauses before entering through glass doors.

mike

Listen, it may not look like Teddy's place, but this ain't the Ivy League either. You can't fuck up around here. You gotta play on your belly.

worm

Sure. 'Course, Chief.

mike

No, I'm serious. You know I got nothing against the way you help yourself. But the guys here are fast company. They'll spot every move, and you won't just get a finger up your spine.

worm

Fine, already.

They enter the lobby and make a left down a flight of stairs.

int. door—same

Mike and Worm stand in front of a steel security door. A small camera films them from a corner above. A magnetic click unlocks the door and they step in.

int. chesterfield club—same

Just inside the door a small sign identifies the club. There is a laquered reception counter with a computer terminal on it.

A young woman steps out from behind the desk. She is PETRA, late twenties, short, dark hair, friendly but with an edge of reserve. Around her neck is a panic button.

petra
Michael McDermott. How you doin', Mike? The computer tried to delete you last week, but I knew you'd be back.

mike
Well, I'm not, but good to see you, Petra. This is Les Murphy, he's like my brother.

Worm extends a hand.

worm
Call me Worm.

petra
Hey.

The phone rings and Petra steps back behind the desk to answer it.

Mike and Worm take in the club. It has a pool table, a large-screen television tuned to ESPN, and several poker tables, though only one game is going on in the far corner.

worm
What's with the necklace on her?

mike
They're wired right in to the Ninth Precinct. They got 'em on the payroll.

Petra rejoins them.

mike
What're they playing?

petra
Twenty-forty forced rotation is the only game going right now.

Mike scopes the game longingly.

mike
Is that fat Greggie sitting twenty-forty now? The game's that soft?

petra
Yeah, it's a real live game. Are you guys going to play?

Mike hesitates, his eyes never leaving the table.

worm
Have a seat, Mike. We'll take this room apart.

Mike gives Worm a stare.

mike
Not gonna happen. I told you, one-time thing. I'm off it, man.

worm
Fucking shame. All right, go runnin' home to her.

mike
Sure, Worm, I will. Take care of 'im, Petra.

Mike takes off.

worm
Girl's got a hold of 'em, I guess. . . .

petra
That's not so bad, is it?

worm

Depends on the grip.

Worm looks around the place again, sizing it up.

worm

So, twenty-forty, huh? Gimme two grand.

Petra squints at him.

petra

On the finger?

worm

Yeah, take care of me. . . . Mikey's good for it, right?

She moves to get the chips.

int. hallway—later

Mike approaches his door, remembers the cigarette still dangling from his lip and gets rid of it.

int. mike's apartment—same

Mike comes through the door, as quietly as possible. Jo, however, sits at the kitchen table with a cup of coffee in front of her.

jo

Reunion run a little late?

mike

Couldn't call. Didn't want to wake you.

He walks to her and puts a hand on her shoulder. Her motion to twitch it off is almost imperceptible.

jo

I wasn't sleeping, Mike. . . . Anyway, change quick, we'll share a cab.

44

mike
Know what, Jo? Go 'head without me. I need a shower, you can cover for me if I miss a little of the Mulligan meeting.

He throws his jacket over a chair and starts taking off his shirt. Jo scrutinizes him.

jo
At least give me a story. Tell me you were out drinking till you threw up or even getting lap dances over at Scores . . .

mike
Yeah, I was entertaining Worm.

jo
Uh-huh.

He stops, looks at her.

mike
What can I say? I owed it to him.

jo
So you were nowhere near a card game?

mike
No . . . I was nowhere near a card game.

Mike's expression is blank, Jo's pained.

jo
Shower quick, I'll wait for you, we'll go to the meeting together.

int. bathroom—same

Mike walks into the bathroom, undresses, and steps into the shower.

Jo enters as the room grows steamy. She silently picks up his pants and discovers the money roll in his pocket. She sets it on the edge of the sink and leaves without a word.

int. cafeteria—later

Jo sits at a table going over notes with the moot trial team. They are GRIGGS and KELLY. Griggs is unshaven with luggage under his eyes; Kelly, straight reddish hair and plaid skirt. All are smoking copiously.

jo

The most important thing to remember is to be respectful to the judges, but not obsequious—

kelly

Now wait a minute, make sure to be deferential—

Mike walks up and interjects.

mike

Gene Marinacci won't buy "deferential."

griggs

Oh, I see. It's "Gene," is it? I knew there's a reason you're lead counsel, and it's got nothing to do with your punctuality.

Mike sits down.

mike

Sorry. Couldn't find a cab.

Mike gives Jo a look. She blanks him.

jo

Fine. So when you give the opening remarks be sure to stick to the fact pattern, and make sure you have the right cites. Use book cites, not Lexis—

Joey Knish, looking uncomfortable and out of place, walks up behind Mike.

knish

I don't mean to interrupt you future magistrates and noblemen, but I need a word . . . Hey, Jo, long time.

jo

How are you, Knish?

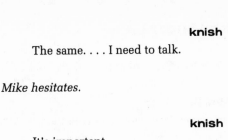

knish

The same. . . . I need to talk.

Mike hesitates.

knish

It's important.

mike (to group)

I'll be right back.

Mike gets up and walks away with Knish. The group is a little annoyed.

kelly

I'll act as lead counsel. . . .

jo

We were about take a break anyway, Kelly, no big deal.

griggs

Coffee time . . .

int. hall—same

Mike and Knish stand in the hall outside the cafeteria.

knish

What're you thinking?

mike

The hell're you talking about?

knish

You're leaking all over the place, Mikey. You're on tilt. How could you bring this guy, this *Greek dealer*, Worm, down to the club?

Students and faculty move in and out of the cafeteria near them.

mike

Look, we can't talk here. . . .

ext. across the street—a bit later

Mike and Knish walk toward some benches across from the law school.

knish

The guy's a cheat, he always has been. Right now he's over there at Chesterfield's ruining your reputation with every lousy second he deals.

mike

Shit. I told 'im. Anybody else see?

knish

Nobody "saw"—I heard it. Snapping sound gave it away. I didn't know him I might not have noticed. But I turn around and see him there with that mechanic's grip, and I know.

mike

Did you give him the office?

knish

Yeah, I tried to warm him, but he looked right through me.

mike

Shit. I better go get him.

Mike zips his jacket, gets ready to leave. Knish sits on the bench.

knish

Sit a while. He's okay now. Most of those Georges're on the tail
end of a thirty-six-hour session and can't see straight. But if he's
still there when Roman and Maurice start their game, he's gonna
wish he was still inside.

mike

No, I gotta go get him. . . .

Knish shrugs.

knish

I unnerstand, I unnerstand.

int. chesterfield club—later

*Worm, shuffling a deck, sits with ROMAN and MAURICE, as well as four
OTHER PLAYERS. Roman is thirty-four, black hair, lambskin sport coat, gold
on pinky, wrist and neck. Maurice, forty-eight, curly gray hair, white
stonewashed denim ensemble, and a gaudy diamond watch.*

They play with the big money—black and gold checks.

(v.o.) mike

Amarillo Slim, the greatest proposition gambler of all time, held
to his father's maxim, You can shear a sheep many times, but skin
him only once. This is a lesson Worm's never bothered to learn.
He's already got them stuffed and mounted over his fireplace, and
he's going for more. If he thinks they're stewing now, wait till they
find out how he beat them.

Roman speaks to Maurice in Russian.

worm

Hey, guys, English only at the table—no Russian.

roman

What?

worm

If you want to see the last card you're gonna stop speaking fucking
Sputnik.

roman

Da, motherfucker.

maurice

He worries we might work together.

worm

Yeah. Look, I'm sure you're just talking about pierogies and snow and shit. . . . Last card coming.

Worm deals the seventh card. Bets go in. Worm's board shows two jacks.

worm

Just the jacks . . .

Maurice shows two pairs, tens and sixes. He prepares to take the pot. Worm flips over his other cards and shows a pair of sevens.

worm (apologetic)

. . . and the sevens.

He smiles and rakes in the pot. Roman and Maurice are livid.

maurice

Motherfucker, slow rolling me like that. You said "just jacks."

worm

Hey, hey. It's *cards speak.* I figured you read me for the sevens.

Worm adds to his stacks, which are now towering.

maurice

Fuck.

Maurice slams his fist on the table and throws his cards into the air. Roman pitches his hand into the muck with similar venom.

Mike enters, a little out of breath. He crosses the room and arrives at the table.

mike

Hey Roman, Maurice.

roman

Mike. You here to play? We need some new blood. They're putting the fucking bracelet on me tomorrow for four months, and I'm already stuck two racks.

He follows this with heated Russian obscenities shared with Maurice.

mike

Have a good rest. (TO WORM) Cosmonaut, c'mere, get some air. . . .

Worm shrugs and organizes his checks. He begins to get up reluctantly, then looks at his chips.

mike

Leave it. It's fine.

Worm looks at his opponents and gestures to his checks.

worm

I counted these. . . .

Mike and Worm head for the door.

ext. street—day

Worm buys a bear claw pastry from a food cart in front of the club.

mike

Where're you at?

worm

Pumped up eight G's. Ready to go on a run when you came along. . . .

Mike takes in this fact.

mike

All right. Listen to me, you're in town five minutes, you already have a sign on your back.

worm

That prick Knishes. Sees all the angles, never has the stones to play one.

Worm throws his bear claw in a garbage can with disgust.

mike

Guy hasn't had to work in fifteen years, Worm.

worm

What he does—grinding it out on his leather ass—that is work.

mike

I thought so, too. Now, I know what work is. . . . Speaking of which, why're you even playing at all? Don't you have to at least look for a job to stay out? Or are you just gonna go back to printing those credit cards? Go away again?

worm

I wasn't printing 'em, just distributing them.

Worm wipes his hands off on his leg.

worm

And I'm never going back. So whattaya want me to do?

mike

Think long term for once. Be smart. Everyone in here keeps books. You get listed as a mechanic, even if you don't get the shit beaten out of you, you won't be able to get action anywhere in New York. It's bad business.

Worm shakes his head with admiration for Mike. His facade wavers.

worm

Fucking Mikey, always seeing the big picture. . . . I can't do what you do, you know? Bust games straight up, or work. This is how I live. You know me, I find a mark, I take him.

mike

I *do* know you. You're the guy who taught me how to play the angles. But right now *you're* the one with your nose open.

Mike puts a hand on Worm's shoulder.

mike

Worm, I'm not just preaching to you here, but these two aren't rabbits. Roman and Maurice are Russian outfit guys. Maybe not so bad as KGB, but nobody you want to fuck with, either.

Worm is chagrined.

worm

Shit.

mike

It's not too late. You go in there and lose their fucking money back. You hear me? Nice and easy. Catch a run of real bad cards. Make it look good.

worm

Yeah? And then? What do I do for money?

Mike thinks about it for a minute.

mike

Take a trip to the suburbs. Find a nice dentist's game or something. Go back to Swan Meadows and play in that golf pros' game. . . .

worm

Yeah, yeah, good idea. Definitely.

Worm looks suitably serious.

worm

Lemme go in and do this. Meet me at Stromboli's in about an hour.

mike

I can't. I have a meeting and later I'm out to Queens and load the fucking truck.

worm

I see. . . .

They turn and part company.

mike
Make it look good. . . .

int. armstrong's tenth avenue—later

Jimmy Armstrong's joint is wood paneled, with a long, friendly bar. Several students and after-work types populate the place. Jo sits amongst them. Mike enters the bar.

jo
Petrovsky waited and waited. So did the group.

mike
Looked all over for you.

jo
Didn't want to be found.

mike
Jo, I missed one meeting—

jo
I don't care about the meeting. You know why I left this morning? I saw that gangster's roll in your pocket. That only means one thing with you.

mike
It's not what you think.

jo
Who am I, young Mary bimbo? You lie right to my face like this. Old days, you never lied. You lost everything, but at least you never lied.

ext. tenth avenue—same

Mike tries to keep pace with Jo striding down Tenth Avenue.

mike
Jo, it was hardly a real game. More like Wiffle ball.

She turns to him.

Funny, I can't remember the last time someone busted out playing Wiffle ball.

mike

Point is, I couldn't lose.

jo

I've heard that one before. Look Mike, I watched you lose every dime you had, and I was still there. But I can't stay for this.

mike

For what?

jo

To watch you go all-in again.

mike

Who's all-in? There're more out cards than dead cards in this deck. First time in my life I can say that.

jo

You counting me?

mike

'Course I'm counting you. Mostly I'm counting you.

jo

Well, I'm no out card, this is my life.

mike
Our life. Exactly. How's one night of cards changing that?

jo
How it starts. One night here, skip a meeting there, next thing I know you're lying to me and rounding again.

mike
You used to like the excitement.

jo
Things were different then.

Mike takes her by the arm, stops her.

mike
C'mon, Jo, I'd walk through the door with winnings, you're there on the bed counting it with me. The trips, the comp rooms. You were booking us out to the World Series at Binion's in April . . .

jo
That was the beginning, and it was a lot of fun. But everything's fun at the beginning. Now I've learned some things. I thought we both did. I guess I was wrong.

Mike starts pacing around anxiously.

mike
You know, this morning I felt like shit for lying to you. But last night, when I sat down, I was James Coburn throwing knives in *The Magnificent Seven.* Cool under fire. I could feel my skin tingling and my fucking blood bubbling, but looking at me, you'd never even know I cared. They were coming for me, but I was ready. I knew exactly what to do. I mean I felt alive for the first time since I got broken at KGB's joint. Can't you understand that?

Jo holds up her hand to try and stop him.

jo
Understand? You just said you felt alive for the first time sitting at a fucking card table. What's that supposed to make me understand?

mike
What I meant—

She walks away.

int. chesterfield's desk—same

Worm stands across the desk from Petra. She is cashing him out.

petra
So, it's ten grand total. I'll take back the two we lent you, and just give you the white meat.

worm
You know what? Give me all ten.

petra
Usually credit players only leave with their profit. Otherwise the juice starts. Five points a week, on Mike.

worm
Fine, we'll owe you.

Petra hesitates, but finally complies and starts counting out hundreds.

ext. billy's topless, sixth avenue—night

Estab. Shot.

int. billy's topless—same

Worm sits in the run-down strip bar. Stringy-haired DANCERS sway listlessly on the stage. A humorless man approaches. He is GRAMA, grimness walking in an overcoat.

grama
I heard you was out.

worm
Hey, Grama. You looking for your old job? I could use you around. Come see me next month, I'll have something for you. . . .

grama

I got some bad news, Worm, I'm out on my own now.

worm

Yeah? Imagine that.

grama

Lot of angry people when you went away. Lot of people were mad.

worm

That's what I'm talking about. It's real tough—

grama

People always coming up to me asking if I could help, asking if I
knew where to find you. It got me to thinking.

worm

So you're thinking now.

*Grama absorbs the insult. Then he grabs Worm by the back of the head and
slams his face into the drink rail in front of him. Worm is dazed.*

*Grama jerks Worm out of his seat by his collar and throws him into the men's
room.*

int. men's room—same

*In one stall a CHUNKY DANCER, purple dress pulled down, is favoring a
boozed-up CUSTOMER.*

grama

Get the fuck outta here.

They clear out in a hurry, Grama's foot moving them along.

*Grama treats Worm to a few gutshots. Worm gasps for air. Recovering, he puts
a cigarette in his mouth, tries to light it.*

grama

Here's what I'm thinking. Instead of owing fifteen grand spread
out to five guys, you owe thirty to me.

58

worm

The fuck you talking about, thirty?

Grama helps the cigarette out of Worm's mouth with a slap.

grama

The *fuck* am I talking about? You know, I think you learned some bad manners inside. Picked up a dirty mouth. Lemme clean it for you.

Grama slams Worm's head into the sink. Runs water on it.

grama

Now here's how it is: thirty and the juice is still running.

Grama lets go of Worm.

worm

Ah . . . You were like my partner, Grama. . . .

grama

No, no, I was your lackey. But I learned some things. I, uh, consolidated your outstanding debt.

worm

Where'd a guy like you get the scratch for a move like that? You've been rolling fags in the Village again—

Grama smacks him again.

grama

Still a wiseass. Unbelievable.

Grama shakes his head.

grama

No, what I did was go partners with an old friend of yours. Teddy KGB backed me.

Worm is taken aback.

worm

KGB—doesn't he have enough muscle? When did he decide to put you under his flag?

grama

Soon as he heard your name. He was real excited by the prospect. Besides, you can never have too much muscle.

worm

So you bought me up, huh, Grama?

grama

Yeah, real sweet deal, too. Thirty cents on the dollar. Not a lot of faith in you out there in the business community.

worm

And now you're a banker.

grama

Not exactly. I don't have to tell *you* my collection methods.

Worm looks a little peaked.

worm

I know, I know. Look, I'll speak to you real soon. I'll have it for you, like next week—

Worm tries to get away, but Grama puts a meaty hand on his chest and pushes him back.

grama

I figured that. So I'll just take what you have on you.

Worm stares at Grama's impassive face, pulls out his fat roll of money, and hands it over.

int. sullivan's bar—night

A small, quiet bar-restaurant resembling an English pub. Dean Petrovsky sits alone at a back corner table reading the newspaper. He has a glass of gin in front of him and they've left him the bottle as well.

Mike enters, spies Petrovsky, and goes over to his table.

mike

Mind if I sit?

Petrovsky gestures at a chair and Mike sits.

petrovsky

Well, Michael, that was a nifty trick the other night. At that point
Marinacci and the D.A. were ready to cut cards for your services.
. . . Of course it was a different trick altogether, that disappearing
act you pulled at your group's meeting today.

mike

That's why I'm here.

Petrovsky takes a Pall Mall from his pack and lights it.

petrovsky

Your Jo, she's a good one. She tried to cover for you. Kelly, on the
other hand, was gunning hard to replace you as lead counsel.

mike

I guess I owe an explanation. . . .

petrovsky

Not to me. I'm sure there's good reason you left. You'll have to
work hard to prepare, and smooth things out with the others. . . .

mike

All right, then. I understand. Thanks for your time. . . .

Mike starts to rise, but Abe waves him down.

petrovsky

Stay. Take a drink, Michael.

mike

What are you having?

petrovsky

Gin, always gin.

Mike takes a glass off an adjacent table and pours himself a drink.

petrovsky

I know a magician's never supposed to tell his secrets, but let me ask you—

mike

I'm no magician.

petrovsky

So if it's not magic, how did you know what they held?

Mike takes a sip of the warm gin and grimaces.

mike

Combination of things. I watched as the cards came out. That's an old habit for me. Like breathing. I saw Marinacci flinch when the three hit green.

petrovsky

You watched the cards?

mike

I watched the cards *also,* but I watched the players reacting to the cards. I knew the D.A. made two pair the same way I knew Kaplan missed his flush, by following their eyes when they checked their river cards. Their faces told me everything.

petrovsky

So you watch the man? I never thought I had to calculate so much at cards.

Mike takes a Pall Mall and puts it in his mouth.

mike

Most important thing—premium hands. You only start with jacks or better split, nines or better wired, three high cards to a flush. If a bet's good enough to call, you're in there raising. Tight but aggressive. And I mean aggressive. That's your style, Professor. Always calculate, think of it as war.

petrovsky

You are officially never invited to our game again.

mike

Don't blame ya. Put a guy like me in a weak game like that, the cards themselves hardly matter. A fish acts strong, he's bluffing, acts meek, he has a hand.

Abe ashes his cigarette.

petrovsky

You know, Michael, it's the same in my avocation. In the courtroom, you'd be surprised how often it comes down to your ability to evaluate people.

mike

Of course you do have to know something about the law. I guess I should spend some more time studying *that*.

Petrovsky smiles.

petrovsky

Let me tell you a story. For generations, the men of my family have been rabbis. In Israel and before that in Europe. It was to be my calling. I was quite a prodigy, Mike, the pride of my yeshiva. The elders said I had a forty-year-old's understanding of the Midrash when I was twelve. By the time I was thirteen though, I knew I could never be a rabbi.

mike

Why not?

petrovsky

Because for all I understood of the Talmud, I never saw God there.

This sends Abe reaching for his drink. Mike refills his glass.

mike

You couldn't lie to yourself.

petrovsky

I tried. Because I knew people were counting on me.

Mike sips his drink.

                         mike
But in the end, yours was a respectable choice.

                       petrovsky
Not to my family. My parents were destroyed by my decision. My
father sent me away to New York to live with distant cousins. . . .
Eventually I found my place, my life's work.

                         mike
What then?

                       petrovsky
I immersed myself fully. I studied the minutiae and learned
everything I could about the law. I believed it was what I was born
to do.

                         mike
Your parents ever get over it?

                       petrovsky
No. They never understood how I consorted with criminals. How
I defended murderers, rapists, and thieves. They considered what
I did dishonorable. I always hoped I might do something to
change their minds, but they were inconsolable. My father
wouldn't speak to me. They died before I became a teacher.

                         mike
And you'd still make the same choices?

                       petrovsky
What choice, Michael? The last thing I took from the yeshiva is
this: We can't run from who we are. Our destiny chooses us.

The men sit huddled together with their thoughts and the gin.

ext. mike's building—later

*Worm is pacing the stoop, smoking nervously, when Mike arrives. Worm is a
little banged up.*

                         worm
Hey, kemosabe.

mike

Hell happened to you?

worm

Cut myself shaving. Ran into a door. What do ya wanna know? . . .
Can I come in?

mike

Uh, sure, 'course. Tone it down though, things haven't been that
smooth on the homefront. . . .

worm

Tone what down, motherfucker?

mike

Great. Forget it.

They enter the building.

int. mike's apartment—same

*Mike and Worm walk through the door to a quiet apartment. Jo is gone, along
with the kitchen table, several appliances, and couch.*

worm

The fuck? You been robbed.

mike

Not exactly.

                              worm

    She's gone, huh?

Worm starts looking around.

                              worm

    You don't seem surprised.

Mike shakes his head.

                              mike

    You won't find any note. She's not the type to leave one. I always
    told her she'd be a good player. She'd know when to release a
    hand the minute it couldn't win.

                              worm

    Smart girl.

                              mike

    Yeah, she's got plenty . . .

*Mike sit-slumps into a kitchen chair—one of the few pieces of furniture that
is his and remains.*

                              mike

    Damn it, I knew I couldn't bluff her. . . .

Worm sits in a chair across from Mike.

                              worm

    Bluff her? Shit, man, you can never trust 'em. Look at you—you
    domesticate yourself, take yourself out of the life. You walk the
    fucking line. You sacrifice for her, man, and then she's gone. It's
    like the saying goes, if life's a poker game, then women are the
    rake, man, women are the rake.

                              mike

    What saying is that?

                              worm

    I don't know, there oughtta be one.

worm

Know what always cheers me up when I'm feeling shitty?

mike

What's that?

worm

Rolled-up aces over kings.

mike

That so?

worm

Check-raising stupid tourists, and taking fat pots off of them calling stations.

mike

Yeah?

worm

Stacks and towers of checks.

mike

I see.

Worm looks around for a place to ash his cigarette, decides on the palm of his hand, then dumps it on the floor and wipes his hand on his leg.

worm

Five hundred dollar freeze-outs all night at the Taj . . . where the sand turns into gold.

Mike stands up.

mike

Fuck it. Let's go.

worm

Serious?

mike

Yeah, I'm serious. Let's do it.

Worm's dreams have come true.

worm

Now we're talking.

ext. atlantic city expressway—night

Mike and Worm roll down the road in one of Hertz's finest. They pass beneath the blue overpass sign that reads WELCOME TO ATLANTIC CITY, AMERICA'S FAVORITE PLAYGROUND.

Ahead of them are the towering neon monoliths along the boardwalk.

ext. taj mahal hotel & casino—same

The rental car pulls up in front of the establishment.

int. taj mahal lobby—casino time

The bang and clatter of games of chance, the lurid lighting and gold mirrors, *the bracing, high-oxygen air, and the burned-out dream chasers give the place that Gomorrah of the East feel.*

Matt and Worm walk past banks of slots and video poker machines toward the card room.

(v.o.) mike

The poker room at the Mirage in Vegas is the center of the poker universe. Doyle Brunson, Johnny Chan, Phil Helmuth—the legends—consider it their office. Every couple of days a new millionaire shows up wanting to beat a world champion. Usually they go home with nothing but a story. Down here, the millionaires are scarce or they're playing craps, but there's still plenty of money for the taking. In fact, on the weekends you can't get a game in the city, because all the New York rounders are taking care of the tourists here.

int. poker room—same

Mike and Worm step up to a cage in front of the poker room. Lists of games and openings are displayed by overhead projectors.

A large, smoky room holding seventy-five poker tables is bustling at half capacity. The crowd's attire is that of a Bowling for Dollars *contestant call.*

Shiny-suited pit bosses communicate by walkie-talkie and microphone, calling out players' initials when seats are available. Horse racing is broadcast on large screens in the back of the room.

int. poker table—same

Mike and Worm stop before reaching their appointed table.

worm

You know what? You play. I'm gonna attend to certain other needs. . . .

mike

Good, I was starting to get worried about you. I thought maybe the boys upstate brought about some changes.

worm

Don't even joke about that.

Worm turns up his collar and stalks off.

Mike continues to his table and sits. At the table are a few familiar faces—Zagosh, Savino, Petra—as well as a guy with a slight tic named GUBERMAN, and another called FREDDY FACE.

Mike puts down some money and the dealer gives him checks.

dealer
Changing five hundred. Good luck, sir.

mike
Beautiful. Welcome to The Chesterfield South. I come all the way to Atlantic City just to look at you mugs.

Greetings are murmured to Mike.

petra
Twice in one week. For someone who doesn't play, you spend a lot of time in card rooms.

dealer
Ten-twenty Hold 'Em. Collection. Pay your time.

All the players put two checks in front of them.

There is a delay before playing as a pit boss brings over a sealed plastic bag containing a box with two decks of cards in it. The dealer makes the decks.

zagosh
Ponies. Why do you still mess around with the ponies? It's for suckers. Even D. Wayne's horses lose. If you gotta gamble, you come here or to Chesterfield's. But to just throw your money away . . . you're like a regular degenerate or something.

savino
This isn't gambling. No real risk of a loss here.

Zagosh and Savino post their blinds. The dealer is ready and gives the first two cards to each player.

guberman

You know, Savino, I think you like to owe. No, you need to owe. It's heroin to you.

petra

No, not heroin, he's like those guys who pay top dollar to get their dicks tied up with twine—he can only get off when he's squeezed.

All the players laugh. Just then Knish walks over to the table and puts his hands on Mike's shoulders.

knish

This is what I like to see. Mike McDermott where he belongs, sitting with the scumbags, telling jokes, dragging the occasional pot.

Bets are called around to Freddy Face. He's a middleweight with a gray pompadour and bushy mustache. He stacks his checks in a nearly despondent manner. He bets before he speaks, putting a few checks in.

freddy face

Occasional? Like my ex-wife *occasionally* went out with other men.

knish

Forget her, Face. . . . Now, I was gonna actually try and make some real money tonight, but in honor of Mike's Ali-like return to the ring, I'll sit with you all for a while.

petra

Don't do us any favors, Knish. They're about to go to the board to fill these seats. Call.

Knish sits down anyway. Zagosh smoothly puts in his checks before he gestures at the table's empty places.

zagosh

If we wanted to try and take each others' rolls we could've stayed back home.

The flop comes and doesn't help anyone much. Petra bets. Everyone folds and she takes it.

A floorman comes over to the table and sticks his hand in the air. Soon, two new players, JASON and CLAUDE, arrive and take their seats. Jason and Claude are typical convention-goers wearing bad leisure suits—Claude's name tag is still on his lapel.

(v.o.) mike

These two have no idea what they're about to walk into. Down here to have a good time, they figure, Why not give poker a try? After all, how different can it be from the home games they've played their whole lives?

Jason and Claude put a few hundred each on the table. The dealer counts the money, the floorman approves of her count, and she exchanges their dollars for checks.

dealer

Five hundred. Good luck, gentlemen.

(v.o.) mike

Luck. All the luck in the world isn't gonna change things for these guys. They're simply overmatched. We're not playing together, but we're not playing against each other, either. It's like the Nature Channel. You don't see piranhas eating each other, do you?

The tone of the table changes. The breezy chatter is put away. The casual observer would never see that the rounders even know one another, much less play together five nights a week.

dealer

Blinds up.

Savino and Petra put in the obligatory bets.

A WAITRESS in a revealing purple and gold outfit stops by. All the rounders pass, she turns to Claude.

claude

Bourbon and water for me, and another Crown Royal for my friend here. . . . I'll call that bet.

mike

Raise. Raise it up.

int. poker table—later

ANGLE ON: Jason and Claude, as they watch their stacks dwindle, as they're chopped up. Soon they stand with apologetic smiles on their faces.

claude
Well, that's it for me. . . .

They leave.

ANGLE ON: The seats being filled by two new suckers, whose stacks dwindle. They leave busted.

The scene becomes a ballet of floormen filling the seats with new players, who leave with nothing.

int. poker table—later

The dealer shuffles between hands when Worm walks up, a new bounce to his step. He sits down between Knish and the Dealer.

Worm reaches across Knish and helps himself to one of Mike's stacks.

worm
Get me started here.

knish (to mike)
Good, that's the way to build the bankroll back up.

savino
Worm, good to see you. Glad you're out. Number's changed of course, new number. Lotta games this weekend, so if you're gonna call and put down some action . . . you're gonna need the new number.

zagosh
Worm, let me ask you, are you allowed in places like this?

worm
What're you, my fucking P.O. now, Zagosh? I didn't think you had a job.

dealer (to worm)

I'm sorry, sir, you can't take chips from another player at the table. . . .

worm

It's all right, honey, we're all friends here.

dealer

I'm sorry, you'll have to buy your chips from me. . . .

Worm leans back, annoyed. He doesn't take money out of his pocket, but instead pulls out a voucher.

worm

Fuck it. Mike, let's hit the noodle bar. I got us comped.

mike

I could have some soup.

Mike gets up.

knish

Oh, look who's treating to a free meal. Don't let that MSG fuck up your head any more than it is, Mikey.

Mike waves him off unconcernedly as they go.

int. noodle bar in the dragon room—later

A seven-seat L-shaped counter tucked away inside the Asian games room of the casino.

Mike and Worm take two seats and hand over Worm's voucher to the ancient Chinese chef. They point out what they want from a short menu.

worm

The hell're you sitting in that rock garden for? Can't get paid in a game that tight. Get serious here.

mike

I like playing with these guys.

worm

These guys have no ambition. Content to sit around ten-twenty splitting two slobs' money five ways. What we need to do is move up to fifty-one hundred, find some rich suckers. A table full of 'em.

mike

I'm not playing short-stacked in a game like that. We'll walk out of here with a grand easy tonight.

worm

A grand. Happy to make a grand. After driving three fucking hours to get here.

mike

Any time I get up with more than I sat down with, it's a good day on the job.

worm

Job? Now you're starting to sound like that sanctimonious prick Knish.

They are served hot tea.

mike

Why don't you calm down.

worm

Oh, I'm calm, real calm.

Worm sips his tea.

worm

You shoulda seen this little skirt I just twirled.

Worm makes some whirring noises and hand gestures that describe the action. A few other diners notice. Mike laughs.

mike

You know something, Worm? You're all elegance and grace.

Large, steaming porcelain bowls of noodle soup are put in front of Mike and Worm. They dig in, slurping noisily.

Pass that hot sauce.

Mike slides a rack of chili sauce over to Worm.

mike

Careful with that, it'll burn a hole right through your stomach.

Worm heaps the red paste into his soup.

mike

So Mr. Nick the Greek, how come you're kiting my checks, instead of helping your own cause?

worm

I'm on empty, that's why.

mike

Tapioca again? How much was the hooker?

He takes a loud slurp.

worm

Please, Mike, "relaxation therapist." But that's not where it went.

mike

Roman and Maurice? I told you to give back, but come on, you could've kept something for your time.

Worm discards his spoon and picks the bowl up, drinking the broth.

worm

That's not where it went, either. Ran into fucking Grama today.

mike

Yeah?

worm

He wasn't seeking reemployment.

Mike pauses.

mike

Who does he work for?

Worm pauses, looks away.

worm

He's, uh, he's on his own now, buying debt. He relieved me of all my holdings.

mike

That cocksucker. Turncoat bastard. So now you owe *him* the ten.

worm

Not by his math.

mike

How fucking much, Worm?

worm

He's says I owed fifteen. With the juice, I guess it's near double that now. . . .

Worm drinks some more soup.

mike

Why didn't you tell me it was that bad? Let me pay towards it when I could've—

Worm drops his bowl in front of him.

worm

It's my problem. . . . Jesus Christ, I'm gonna have you pay what I owe? I'll have you help me, like we used to. It's why we're here. But I'm no leech.

mike

All right, all right. Of course I'll help. I am helping. . . . But Grama, shit. Maybe we can talk to him. Get you some time off the vig.

Worm shakes his head. He wipes his hands on his pants.

worm

I doubt it. You don't know how he feels about me, man. I wasn't
the most understanding boss.

Mike gives him a pat on the back. They stand up.

mike

Fuck him, we'll figure something out. Let's go.

worm

Could you leave the tip?

Mike gives him a look.

int. city law university—morning

*Mike, pasty faced, unshaven, runs down the hall trying to straighten his tie.
A sheaf of loose papers is stuffed under his arm.*

int. moot courtroom—same

*Resemblant of a classroom converted into a courtroom. Judge Marinacci sits
on panel with Petrovsky and a middle-aged female judge—JUDGE
McKINNON.*

*Behind facing desks are Jo, Griggs, and Kelly, and the OPPOSING TRIAL
TEAM.*

The judges look impatient. The door at the back of the room swings open and Mike enters.

petrovsky
Perhaps we can begin now?

Mike puts his papers on the team desk and sits down.

mike
Sorry I'm late.

jo
You ready?

Mike tries to have a conversation with his eyes. Jo gives him nothing.

judge marinacci
Come to order in the matter of *Slater* versus *New York State Higher Education Services.* The facts have been stipulated, the briefs have been read. Lead counsel for Plaintiff, ah, Mr. McDermott, please proceed with oral arguments now. If that's convenient for you.

Mike stands up, he looks rattled, unprepared.

mike
Yes, sir, Your Honor. Clearly the case that controls the issue at bar is *Texas* versus *Johnson,* which holds. Which holds . . .

Mike thumbs through a folder, unable to locate the information.

judge marinacci
Texas versus *Johnson?* Mr. McDermott, that is a Supreme Court free speech case that has no bearing here. Each group was advised to ignore that aspect of this matter and focus instead on the idea of de facto segregation.

Mike is silent. He looks to the group. Kelly stands up.

kelly
Mr. McDermott has been unreachable, so I'll take over now, if that pleases the court.

judge marinacci

Somebody saying something meaningful would please us a great deal. . . .

Judge Marinacci shoots Petrovsky a look. Petrovsky shrugs. Mike sits down.

ext. city law university—later

The City Law team walks out of the building. Mike looks haggard, shell-shocked. Griggs whacks him across the back.

griggs

Well, that was impressive. Usually you know what the case is about when you give an opening statement.

mike

Guys, what can I say? I was less prepared than I thought—

kelly

Worked out great for me, McDermott. I think I actually impressed Marinacci. . . .

Mike stops walking. They continue on, except Jo.

mike

Jo, we need to talk about this. You moved pretty fast here.

jo

You make it sound like it was my decision.

mike

Wasn't mine. I come home and you're gone. How could you give up on me so quick?

jo

Mike, I learned it from you. You always told me this was the rule. Rule number one: Throw away your cards the moment you know they can't win. Fold the fucking hand.

mike

Well, this is us we're talking about, not some losing hand a cards.

She takes this in.

                              jo

Yeah, I know exactly what we're talking about.

                              mike

So this is the last of it?

                              jo

That's right, Mike, this is where I get off.

                              mike

Jo, you're overreacting. It's not like I'm out running around on
you. Look, I want to make things right.

She half smiles, trying not to break.

                              jo

You know, most of my friends wonder, at least sometimes, if their
husbands or boyfriends cheat on them. I never had to worry about
that, with you the only other woman was poker.

                              mike

Babe, I—

                              jo

I'd say good luck, Mike. But I know it's not about luck in your
game.

She leaves him standing there.

ext. street—later

Mike walks the streets alone, hands in pockets, head down.

ext. sullivan's—night

Mike enters the bar.

int. sullivan's—same

Behind the oak is a strapping English BARTENDER. Mike approaches.

                              mike

Seen Abe Petrovsky?

bartender

Most every day I've worked here. Already been and gone tonight, though. Get you something?

mike

Gin, I guess. I'll have a gin.

The Bartender pours.

int. mike's apartment—later

Mike sits on the floor in front of his small television set and VCR, which now rests on a cardboard box.

ANGLE ON: the television. Two men play poker. A large crowd surrounds the table. One of them is a diminutive Asian named JOHNNY CHAN who sits with his lucky orange in front of him, the other is a young New Yorker, ERIC SEIDEL.

Chan raises his arms in victory—he's just won the World Series of poker. Stacks of cash are poured onto the felt in front of him.

Mike rewinds the tape, the images moving jerkily in reverse. He is ready to watch the moment again when the door buzzer sounds.

int. mike's doorway—same

Mike speaks into the intercom.

mike

Yeah?

ext. front of building—same

Petra stands at the door and speaks into the intercom.

petra

Mike? It's Petra. Can I come up?

The door buzzes and she enters.

int. mike's apartment—same

Mike stands at the door and lets Petra in. She enters, surveys the sparse decor.

petra
Haven't seen the place in a while. . . . Looks about the same.

mike
Yeah.

She looks over his shoulder at the television.

petra
'Eighty-eight World Series, huh? Johnny Chan. Flops the nut straight, and has the discipline to wait him out. He knows Seidel's gonna bluff at it.

mike
Johnny-fucking-Chan.

petra
Look at the control. He knows his man well enough to check it all the way and risk winning nothing with those cards. He owns him.

ANGLE ON: the television. The young man makes the fateful bet.

petra
Poor Seidel. Kid doesn't know what hit him.

They watch Chan flip his cards. Mike shakes his head at Seidel's defeat. He freezes the frame on the carnage.

mike
I know what that feels like. Like a locomotive running through your guts. All the air rushes out of you. You're reeling. . . . Gutshot.

ANGLE ON: the television, where Johnny Chan is awarded stacks of cash money, over 700 thousand dollars' worth, and a gold bracelet for his efforts.

Mike shuts off the television.

mike
Fuck it, you didn't come here to talk about this. What's going on?

petra

Tomorrow's a week.

mike

A week of what?

petra

The first two thousand you owe the Chesterfield.

Mike goes to the kitchenette across the room and gets himself a glass of water from the tap.

mike

Worm.

petra

Strangest thing, he'd just won eight grand, why go on the line behind another two?

Mike keeps his surprise in check. He's inscrutable.

mike

So he beats Roman and Maurice for about eight then?

Petra thinks for a moment.

petra

Yeah. He comes back in after you leave. Sits for like twenty more minutes. And cashes out for the full amount. Maurice hasn't been back since. I think he's been playing 'cross the street. But Worm's been around plenty. He's run you up just under seven grand.

Mike's expression is as mild as if he just heard the weather is partly cloudy.

mike

Do me a favor, put him on his own.

petra

Yeah?

mike

Cut him off.

Mike takes out his roll and counts off a thousand, which leaves him with a few hundred.

> **mike**
> You know I just started coming around again. But here's a thou towards it.

Mike hands her the money and she pockets it.

> **petra**
> Thanks for making it easy, Mike. I'm sorry to be back over here for this reason.

> **mike**
> Don't worry about it.

Petra steps up close to him.

> **petra**
> But I like being here, it's good to see you.

They share a look. She leans closer, puts her hand on his chest. They kiss.

> **petra**
> I could stay. . . .

Mike brushes her hair away from her face, then steps back.

                              mike

No. I'll see you this week, Petra.

She hesitates. Mike moves her toward the door and she reluctantly leaves. He closes the door behind her.

                              mike

Fucking Worm.

He thinks for a moment and puts on his jacket.

ext. building—night

A taxi pulls up and Mike steps out. The cab drives off, Mike looks around, then walks to the back of the darkened building.

ext. back of building—same

Mike climbs up on a Dumpster and pulls himself up to an open transom window.

int. paterson catholic high gymnasium—same

The rhythmic sound of a basketball being dribbled. The squeak of shoes and thump of the ball hitting iron.

Worm is alone in a mostly darkened gym, shooting around.

He is interrupted by the creaking sound of the cantilevered window opening. Worm ducks beneath the bleachers.

Mike climbs in the window above the bleachers and walks down to the gym floor.

ANGLE ON: A sleeping bag, a few belongings, and a lot of White Castle wrappers lying in a corner.

                              mike

I know you're here.

Worm steps out from the bleachers.

worm

Hey, Mikey.

mike

Good thing Grama doesn't know you as well as I do.

Worm sends a bounce pass to him.

worm

Horse? Fifty bucks a letter?

mike

When I win, you gonna pay me with my fucking money?

On the word "money," Mike sends back a brisk chest pass to Worm.

worm

Easy.

Worm throws a chest pass back with very good form.

worm

Step, and snap the thumbs down.

He holds his form for a long moment.

Mike imitates the form, but intentionally sends the ball into the opposite corner of the gym.

worm

All right. We'll work on the accuracy.

Mike kicks the bleachers.

mike

Would you stop fucking around, for five minutes, for once in your goddamned life? You stupid, selfish prick.

worm

Jesus, you sound like my old man.

mike

Yeah, I ought to kick the crap out of you, like he did.

Worm goes after the basketball.

worm

Mikey Boy, 'member the first time we found this place?

Worm starts shooting hoops.

mike

Eleventh grade. We broke in when Tommy Manzy was looking to pound you into oblivion.

worm

Yeah, what was he pissed about?

Mike looks at him, half smiles despite himself.

mike

You fucked his mother.

Worm reflects. He smiles.

worm

Good-looking older woman.

mike

She was that, but you spent a year dodging that sick fuck. Till he pissed off Lostrito and that garbage can fell on his head from thirty floors up.

worm

Crazy times. We were wild then.

mike

Nothing's changed. You were hiding out 'cause of your trouble *then*. You're still hiding out.

worm

Yeah, I remember hiding out plenty, but not behind solo fuckups. I seem to remember a runnin' buddy.

mike

But we got caught back then, the worst that could happen was you catch a beating or get expelled. Now—now you're fixing to go down hard. And it almost seems like you want to.

worm

I'm turning things around. Don't you worry, no garbage can's gonna hit me.

mike

Yeah, you're getting out of the way and it's gonna land on me. See ya later, Worm.

Mike heads for the door. Worm drops the basketball.

worm

Listen, Mike. Listen. Don't leave. I'm sorry about that money. Really. I needed it to get some things going.

Mike turns.

mike

And?

worm

Well, I won't lie to you, there've been some reversals.

mike

Reversals, huh. How much is left?

worm

Nine hundred. I caught a frozen wave of cards, like you read about.

mike

You gotta be kidding me. I think I'm getting *you* outta hock, and I find out *I'm* seven grand in.

worm

Hey, I was feeling lucky. Playing blackjack over at the Horseshoe Club in Brooklyn.

mike

That place is a mitt joint, schmuck. . . .

worm

I thought I could neutralize 'em.

mike

No, you're neutralized. You've really jammed me up here. Seven grand. I can't go any deeper, you're off the tit.

worm

If that's how it's gotta be—

mike

That's not all. You gotta talk to Grama, work something out—

worm

No way. I'm not talking to that Judas son of a bitch.

Mike thinks for a second.

mike

You see any other way?

worm

Shit.

mike

Let's get out of here.

They head for the fire door together, shutting out the light when they reach it.

mike

Time being, it's best you stay with me.

worm

What, and give up the lease on my penthouse?

Worm gestures at his pile of crap in the corner.

mike

You got any other choices?

worm

Think Manzy's mom is still around?

They exit.

ext. building on mott street, chinatown — day

Mike and Worm stand before tenement-style building. The ground floor houses Wo Shu Op Chinese restaurant. To the side of the restaurant is the door to the other floors.

The buzzer panel is ripped out, the lock broken. They enter.

int. bldg. hallway — day

Mike and Worm stand in a gray hallway and knock. The sounds of several deadbolts being thrown, and then the door opens. They step inside.

int. railroad apartment — same

SHERRY has let them in. She is in her late twenties, wearing a polyester camisole and too much foundation. GINA, a petite Asian also in a camisole, sits on a sofa, talks into a phone, and ignores them.

>   sherry
> Hi, boys.

>   mike
> Hello.

>   sherry
> You cops? You look like cops.

>   worm
> We're not cops.

>   sherry
> You want a twirl then?

>   mike
> No. Grama here?

sherry
Oh.

mike
Yeah. Tell him Mike and Worm need a minute.

She vanishes into the recesses of the apartment.

worm
This is not good. I feel like I been remanded again. You sure—

Mike cuts him off with a look at the girl on the couch.

mike
Don't say much. Don't let 'im read your mail.

Sherry calls out to them, and they walk down the hall toward Grama's office.

int. apartment hallway—same

The hall is dimly lit and cramped. They pass several closed doors, behind which muffled sounds of "paid passion" can be heard.

int. grama's office—same

The room is dingy and devoid of charm: several phones and scraps of paper on a desk, and a tatty chair.

The space is populated, though, by two enthusiastic PIT BULLS that leap around Mike and Worm, to their great discomfort.

grama
Hey, Mike. Hey, Worm, it's good you came. Real smart thinking.

worm
Thanks for the endorsement, Grama.

mike
Grama, it's been a long time.

grama (to worm)
So, you brought him along to help carry all my money?

mike

There's no money today.

Grama takes a stance in front of the door. It is now uncomfortably close in the room. The sound of the dogs panting and slobbering can be heard.

grama

No money? There has to be some money.

worm

None.

grama

You owe fifteen grand. I'll take it in three days.

mike

Five grand. In a week. You keep the juice going.

Grama is distracted by one of the pit bulls chewing on the corner of the chair.

grama

Shh, shh. Quiet. You have to catch them in the act.

Mike and Worm are confused as Grama creeps up behind the dog. He pounces on the pit bull, wrestling it to the floor on its back. Grama straddles the dog and puts his face into its muzzle. He speaks sternly and all too intimately.

grama

No. Bad dog. B-a-a-a-d dog.

worm

Jesus Christ.

Grama gets off the cowed animal, who slinks away.

grama

You can't let 'em get away with it, or they think they run the place.
. . . Anyway, where were we?

Mike speaks his terms again, with considerably less confidence.

mike

Five grand. One week. Come on, Grama, we want what you

want—to square this thing. Three days is impossible. Five grand
this week, the rest after that. No one's arguing that you're the man,
so make it a business decision.

Grama considers the proposal. Puffs up at the idea of himself in control.

Worm can't take his eyes off the dog.

> **mike**
> Look, Worm just got out. Put him on a plan—

> **grama**
> No, no. this isn't the Money Store. We aren't negotiating here. I
> tell you how it works.

> **mike**
> Come on Grama, I'm asking here. . . .

Grama looks ready to relent.

> **grama**
> You're looking for grace, Lester? For some charity—

Worm just can't bring himself to keep quiet.

> **worm**
> Fucking charity? I'll never take charity from this fat fuck of an
> errand boy—

> **mike**
> Shut the fuck up, Worm.

Grama glowers.

> **grama**
> Too late for him to shut up. Too fucking late. He ain't getting outta
> here now.

*Grama closes the distance between him and Worm. Mike steps in front and
cuts him off.*

mike

Come on, Grama, he's good for it. He'll get you your money.

Grama stops and glares at them.

grama

If you're saying he's good for it Mike, it's on you, too.

mike

Then it's on me, too.

grama

Fifteen large. Three days. Else I'll start breaking things.

Mike nods.

mike

I hear you.

Grama scrutinizes them.

grama

In that case, you can leave.

Grama opens the door and lets them out.

ext. mott street—day

Mike and Worm hurry through the strange streets.

mike

What the fuck is wrong with you? You're habitual.

worm

I know, I know. Sorry . . . I can't believe I'm going out like this. Fifteen grand in three days—forget it man, we're done.

Mike looks at his friend.

mike

We're not done yet. Fifteen grand? I've gone on rushes that big before.

worm

Come on, Mike. Maybe under optimum conditions. Maybe. But how much you have on you?

mike

About three-fifty.

worm

That puts us at around twelve hundred. What do you think we can do with that? Fucking Lotto?

mike

No, we do what we do.

worm

Like in Princeton?

mike

Nah. We can't sit together. That's too risky in the city. We do it like we used to—you find the games, you scout the games. I sit and mop 'em up.

Worm is hesitant to even hope.

worm

You'd still do that for me?

mike

I have to fucking do it. I'm hanging on the hook right next to you.

Mike pops an unlit cigarette into his mouth.

mike

We have five days. There's the thirty-sixty at The Chesterfield. The Greeks. The four A.M. game in Woodside. You find some more.

worm

You sure you're ready for this?

mike

Lead me to it.

They disappear down the steps to the Canal Street subway station.

int. union hall, west fourteenth street—day

ANGLE ON: A crest reading INTERNATIONAL BROTHERHOOD OF TEAMSTERS AND CHAUFFEURS LOCAL 237.

Mike sits at a large, round table with several teamsters, both regular members—truckers in their working clothes and union officials in suits.

larossa

I'll bet the full amount.

mike

Full amount, huh? Let me look at you.

Mike stares closely into Larossa's face, Larossa meets the stare.

mike

No, I don't think you made it, Larossa. Raise.

Mike pushes in his checks. Larossa waits a tense moment, then folds his hand.

Mike rakes in the pot.

int. chesterfield club—later

Mike sits with some usual suspects and some new faces in the thirty-sixty Hold 'Em.

The board reads 7–S, 5–D, 9–C, 3–H.

ANGLE ON: Mike's hole cards are 6–S, 8–D.

Mike appears hesitant despite his nut straight.

> **mike**
>
> Check it.

> **zagosh**
>
> I'll bet sixty.

> **mike**
>
> Let's see what you have. Raise.

> **zagosh**
>
> Trying to put a move on me, Mike? But I'm not going anywhere. Call.

The river card comes K–C.

> **zagosh**
>
> Sixty.

Mike looks at the board as if he suddenly realizes there's a possible straight out there.

> **mike**
>
> Could you have? You play four–six? I don't think so. Raise.

> **zagosh**
>
> Call.

Zagosh flips over his cards and shows his straight to the seven.

> **zagosh**
>
> I made my straight. Sometimes it's the little ones that do you the most good, Mike. . . .

Mike turns his 6–8 over.

> **mike**
>
> Sorry, Zagosh, you caught the dumb end of it this time. To the nine.

Mike rakes in the pot.

int. gus's smoke shop, woodside avenue —4:00 a.m.

The 4:00 A.M. game goes on in the otherwise closed-for-business smoke shop. Nine of the ten players puff on cigars. Mike has the dead cigarette in his mouth. He looks miserable sucking in all the cigar smoke.

The game is Seven-Stud Hi-Lo, eights or better.

Eisenberg bets, holds up his double corona with admiration.

eisenberg
. . . The Cameroon wrapper on this baby, nice and oily.

Sunshine, a bright-eyed young lady, brandishes her cigar.

sunshine
I don't know. I kinda like this robusto. Hints of pepper and spice, a nice, nutty finish. I'll call. What do you got?

Mike looks fed up as the cards are turned over, but his hand is an ace–5 straight.

mike
I got a wheel. It has earthy tones. A smooth draw, and a good enough kick to win me the High *and* the Low.

Mike rakes it in.

int. back of pluto's diner—day

The din of Greek being shouted and plates banging. Mike is beginning to look exhausted.

The players are Mediterranean-looking, drinking espresso and smoking cigarettes. They practice sophistry by criticizing each other's play.

Mike turns over his cards.

mike
Trip aces.

zizzo

I only have a pair. Jacks.

Mike accesses the pot.

taki (yelling)

What did you think he had, Zizzo? Does he look like a man beaten by jacks?

cronos (yelling)

Jacks are a monster compared to the crap you play, Taki.

taki (yelling)

Fuck you. Fuck you.

cronos (yelling)

Fuck you. Fuck you.

zizzo (meek)

I liked the jacks.

taki (yelling)

Fine, forget it. Deal. Deal. Deal.

Mike shakes his head and shuffles the cards.

ext. swan meadows golf club—day

Rain drenches the lavish golf course.

int. pro shop—same

Mike sits playing poker with colorfully dressed golf pros, caddies, and a few members. He is looking worn, with a growth of beard. They play pot limit Seven-Stud, deuces wild.

Worm is across the room, putting golf balls on the carpet.

johnny gold

The hell, it's only money. I bet.

Mike looks at the cards on the table and at Gold.

mike

Then let's get some more in there. Make it five hundred.

Gold puts his checks in with flicks of his wrist.

johnny gold

Yeah? All right. I raise. Size of the pot.

Worm halts his putting and looks over attentively. A few grand is in the center.

weitz

You sure on that, Goldie? Might want to leave some over for your daughter's riding lessons.

Mike waffles. He mucks his cards.

mike

Take it down.

Gold turns over his cards. He has nothing.

johnny gold

Lookit that, I bluffed out the ringer.

Gold and Weitz high-five and Gold takes the money.

Mike shrugs it off, but Worm steps up and pulls Mike away from the table.

worm

C'mon. Let's go.

Mike is annoyed, but too tired to argue. They head for the door.

johnny gold

What do I always say? Anybody, anytime . . . Assholes . . .

ext. golf course—day

Mike and Worm stand near the first tee box.

worm

The fuck's the matter with you?

mike

I didn't have it.

worm

You didn't have it? Since when do you gotta have it to beat a puke like that out of a pot? A grade-schooler woulda played back at him.

mike

I was prepared to wait him out. Eventually he'd have bluffed at the wrong pot, and I'd have had him.

worm

We don't have the time. You gotta make moves.

mike

The move was folding. You can't lose what you don't put in the middle.

worm

Fuck that. We needed that pot. Where are we at?

mike

I'm too tired to count it.

Mike hands over the bankroll to Worm, who counts it with the crispness of a bank teller.

worm

Seventy-three hundred. Pot you just gave that V-neck sweater would've put us near ten grand. Look at you, one sixty-four-hour session, and you need a nap.

mike

Fuck that. Can't sleep. We don't have the time.

worm

Yeah, yeah. I know what you need.

int. barber shop, seventh avenue—later

Mike and Worm lay back in barber chairs with hot towels covering their faces. They are attended to by two silent BARBERS.

mike

I feel like I'm gonna get whacked sitting here like this.

Barbers take the towels off of their faces and start putting on shave cream. The barbers brandish gleaming straight-edge razors and go to work. Mike and

Worm talk while barely moving their mouths now, trying to get a word in between strokes.

worm
Seventy-three. We have two days to double it.

mike
We'll get close. Look, I'm sure if we're a little short Grama will—

worm
I know a game . . . up in Binghamton. An all-nighter with twelve to sixteen guys. Two tables running. Municipal workers. It's on after they cash their paychecks.

mike
You sure about this? We drive up there we kill five hours each way. . . .

worm
There's fifteen, twenty grand in the room. We only need half that.

The barbers begin wiping off the residual shave cream. Mike sits up refreshed.

mike
Lead me to it.

ext. parking lot of knights of columbus hall—night

Mike and Worm pilot their rental off a rural road into the parking lot. There are a dozen cars there, all state trooper brown-and-whites.

Worm parks the car amongst the others and they climb out.

mike
Municipal workers, huh?

worm
They work for the city.

mike
They work for the state, you idiot. I don't like this at all.

worm

You see any other way?

Mike considers it.

mike

Shit, how am I even supposed to get in this game?

worm

Easy. This guard, Pete Frye, I must've lost ten grand to him over eighteen months. The guy thought I was tuna fish. His nephew plays here. Ask for Sean Frye.

Mike checks his watch.

mike

I figure about eight hours. So be back here by seven, seven-thirty in the morning.

worm

The hell am I gonna do in this town for eight hours? All they have is car washes and liquor stores. I thought I'd come in, sit for a while.

mike

No, Worm. Look around you. We'd have to be nuts to walk in there together. I already have half a mind to leave.

worm

C'mon, I'll play it straight up.

mike

Fine then. You play and I'll be back in eight hours.

worm

All right, all right. I'll find a bowling alley or something. . . .

Worm gets back in the car. Mike walks toward the hall and puts an unlit cigarette in his mouth.

int. knights of columbus hall—same

The place has cheap wood paneling, a vinyl-covered bar kept by a BARTENDER, deer heads on the wall, and Naugahyde chairs surrounding two poker tables. Large bodies of off-duty TROOPERS fill the chairs. Some are in uniform, some are in plaid flannel shirts. They all have mustaches.

Mike's arrival gains some attention.

> **bartender**
>
> Help you?

> **mike**
>
> Looking for Sean Frye.

> **bartender**
>
> That's him over there.

The Bartender points to a man with red hair, crew cut. Mike walks over to him.

> **mike**
>
> Sean Frye? Your Uncle Pete said to ask for you if I was ever up near here.

> **frye**
>
> You one of his "students?"

> **mike**
>
> No. I wasn't inside.

> **frye**
>
> You must know him from hunting then. . . .

> **mike**
>
> Yeah. He beat me for about a grand over the lodge.

> **frye**
>
> Well, that's the buy-in here. We play twenty-forty Stud, grab a seat.

Mike takes his place in the game.

int. poker table—later

Mike has solid stacks in front of him. A hand is being dealt.

(v.o.) mike
Generally, the rule is, the nicer the guy, the poorer the card player. These guys, despite being cops, are real sweethearts. I'm right on schedule, up forty-two hundred. The morning can't get here soon enough.

ANGLE ON: The door. A large patrolman, BEAR, walks into the hall with his arm around Worm. A hail of greetings go up to Bear.

bear
Hey, fellas. Met this guy down the tavern. Says he likes to play a little cards.

Worm is offered a chair by a small officer, VITTER. Two of the others at the table are WHITLEY and OSBOURNE.

vitter
Came to the right place.

Sean Frye offers his hand.

frye
Sean Frye. You met Bear. This is Vitter, Whitley, and Osbourne. This guy's name is Mike.

Mike and Worm shake hands.

worm
I'm Les.

vitter
Deal Les a hand, Whitley.

Cards go out.

int. poker table—later

Mike's stacks are healthy. Worm is appropriately behind. Worm deals the hand.

ANGLE ON: Mike's cards, which are a king showing and two kings underneath.

Osbourne, showing ace of hearts, bets.

osbourne
I like what I have. The bet is twenty.

Mike looks at his cards.

mike
I believe him. Fold.

All eyes are on the next cards dealt, but Mike glares at Worm.

int. poker table—later still

Mike reluctantly posts his ante as the deal comes to Worm again. Cards go out.

ANGLE ON: Mike's cards, which are ace on board with sevens wired underneath.

Since Mike's high with an ace showing, he must act first.

mike

Check 'em.

Hands are checked around, so Mike doesn't have the opportunity to fold.

Worm deals the next card to each player. Upon reaching Mike, he deals him a seven, but two cards jut out obviously from the bottom of the deck.

ANGLE ON: Worm's hand hurries to square the cards, but it's too late.

vitter

Hold on there a fucking second.

Heads raise up around the table and all attention is on Vitter.

vitter

Put the deck down.

worm

What?

vitter

Put down the damned deck.

Worm obeys.

The game at the second table halts and everyone cranes for a look at what's going on. Even the bartender stops pouring.

vitter

Looks like we got ourselves a road gang here.

At this the troopers from the other game get up and surround the table.

All eyes bore into Mike and Worm. Mike's cards are practically glowing neon.

A towering officer from the other table steps in to adjudicate. He is SERGEANT DETWEILER.

detweiler

Hell's going on, Stu?

vitter

This son of a bitch is base dealing and caught a hanger, Sarge.

worm

Base dealing? Hanger? The fuck're you talking about?

detweiler

He's saying you're dealing from the bottom of the deck.

frye

What'd he give him?

vitter

Seven of hearts.

detweiler

You boys professionals? You "working"?

mike

No, I—

detweiler

Don't answer. Cards speak for now. Long as that seven didn't help you, we'll listen to what you have to say. Turn his cards, Whitley.

Whitley moves to flip Mike's undercards. Mike looks ill, as if he just wants to disappear.

The cards are turned—two black sevens. He's got trips.

detweiler

One last thing.

Detweiler leans across the table and picks up the deck. He holds it up, showing the bottom card to all in the room: ace of diamonds.

The room is completely silent for a moment.

worm

Guess you'll be readin' us our rights then?

vitter

Yeah.

A chair scrapes against the floor, and the tables are upset as Mike and Worm are jerked from their seats. Mike's cigarette falls from his mouth.

Huge, meaty blows rain down on them. Fists and feet thrown by underpaid but well-trained men who don't receive much respect for the job they do.

Just as it seems to have subsided, a new wave of punches descends. Everyone gets a piece of Mike and Worm.

As Mike and Worm lay on the floor bleeding, several hands rifle their pockets, taking every loose dollar they have.

ext. parking lot—night

Mike stirs on the ground. The lot is empty but for their rental car. He groans as he comes to a sitting position.

mike
Jesus.

He crawls over to Worm and gently tries to bring him around.

mike
Worm? Worm? Les, you all right?

Finally Worm comes to.

worm
Mike . . .

mike
Yeah?

worm
You should've played the kings.

Mike leans back.

mike
Asshole.

worm
I know, I know.

They halfheartedly pat at their pockets.

mike
Everything. They took it all.

Worm clutches at his shoe. He pulls out a few hundreds.

worm
Three hundred. That's all I've got.

Mike takes out his cigarettes. He has his folded hundred. Mike spits out a mouthful of blood. His eyes are blackened.

worm
I can't believe I caught a fucking hanger. . . . That never happens.

Mike tries to stand, but sways back to a sitting position.

mike
Man, these guys were thorough. Anything broken on you?

Worm passes his cigarette to Mike and probes around his face with his fingers.

worm
Maybe my nose.

mike
What were you fucking thinking in there? I had 'em.

worm
I was trying to give you an edge.

Mike doesn't respond.

worm
I said I'm sorry. I took my shot, and missed. Happens.

mike

Happens all the time around you, Worm.

worm

Happens to you too, Mike. You're the one took that big fall before
I came out. You had about three fucking dollars in your pocket
when I saw you—

mike

Fuck you. That's different—

worm

It's always different for you, huh? Your shot is somehow fucking
noble, mine's not worth shit. You think you're the only one with
ambitions.

mike

Yeah? What's your ambition?

worm

You know . . .

mike

No, I don't. You fucking tell me.

worm

. . . Ah, I don't fucking know. . . . I don't think like that.

mike

You don't think.

worm

Exactly. I just try and get by. That's all I can do now. You weren't
in there with me. . . . The noise, the constant fucking noise. Iron
doors banging. You never sleep, you only wait till morning. We're
just different now, man. *You're* looking down the road. Always
figuring. Calculating the odds, playing your man. *You're* going
pro. Sitting in the Mirage, rubbing elbows with Johnny-fucking-
Chan. *You* think you can beat the game, straight up. I know it can't
be done. I know the only way is if you have an edge. That's my
way.

Mike hauls himself to his feet.

mike

Okay, what's our edge now? We owe fifteen grand in a day. How do we play this, Ace?

Worm gets up.

worm

This? This you know. We fold the fucking hand. Get the fuck outta Dodge. Steer wide of New York. Plenty of places guys like us can quietly earn a living. Be back on our feet in no time.

mike

Guys like us? *I'm* not living like that. Go back to New York, talk to Grama, find someone to stake me—

worm

Talk to Grama? Well, it's not just Grama.

mike

What're you talking about? You said Grama was on his own.

worm

Well, truth is Teddy KGB bankrolled that cock-diesel psycho.

Mike looks surprised, but only for a moment.

mike

KGB. So you've fucked us right up the ass, Worm.

worm

Yeah, now you see what I mean. Highway time.

Mike spits out some blood.

mike

I'd rather face it now. If they're gonna do me worse than this, I want to see it coming.

Worm reflects on this.

worm

Time to go Greyhound, Mikey. You with me?

mike

No, I'm not, Worm. Not this time.

There is silence. They stare at each other. Mike turns and starts walking away.

Worm zips his jacket. He calls after Mike.

worm

At least you're rounding again. You should thank me for that.

Mike keeps walking.

ext. mott street apartment—day

Mike walks in.

int. building hallway—same

Mike walks down the hall.

(v.o.) mike

Fold or hang tough. Call or raise the bet. These are decisions you
make at the table. Sometimes the odds are stacked so clear there's
only one way to play it. Other times, like holding a small pair
against two over cards, it's six to five, or even money, either way.
Then it's all about feel, what's in your guts.

ANGLE ON: His fist knocking on the door. It swings open.

int. apartment hallway—same

*Mike stands at one end. Grama steps from his office, backlit, and stands at
the other end. They are thirty feet apart.*

grama

Look at you.

mike

Yeah, look at me.

grama

Come in.

mike

Nah.

grama

Where's your friend?

mike

Oh, he's gone.

grama

So you've got the money?

mike

A little short.

Grama moves down the hall closing the distance.

grama

How short?

mike

The whole way.

grama

Must be some kinda story.

mike

I don't figure you want to hear it.

grama

Where's your friend?

mike

He's really gone.

grama

Then I don't want to hear it.

Grama moves even closer.

116

You see I can't pay.

I see you're banged up pretty good.

Yeah.

Never should have vouched for that scumbag.

Mike shrugs.

Maybe not.

You're leaving me no outs here.

Why?

Can't trust you two aren't playing me.

I'm not the one working with a partner.

Grama gets right up in Mike's face.

You wanna take it up with KGB, go ahead. Otherwise, you have a
day and a half, or this'll feel like a Swedish massage.

Mike backs out to the hallway and leaves the apartment.

int. russian baths—night

*Mike walks through a bathhouse. Large eastern European MEN in towels soak
in tubs.*

Mike sticks his head into the steam room and waves Knish out.

As Knish steps out and puts on a robe, he sees Mike's condition.

> **knish**
> You look like Duane Bobick after one round with Norton. Fuck
> happened to you?

Mike shrugs.

> **mike**
> Worm.

> **knish**
> That motherfucker. When're you gonna listen?

> **mike**
> I'm listening.

> **knish**
> Cops get involved?

> **mike**
> Yeah, they did.

> **knish**
> Whattaya need? Five hundred, a grand?

> **mike**
> I need fifteen thousand dollars.

> **knish**
> Fifteen? . . . I need a blow job from Christy Turlington. Get the
> fuck outta here, fifteen thousand dollars . . .

Mike takes it in.

> **mike**
> Seriously, Joey, what can you do for me? Five hundred isn't even
> gonna get me started.

knish

Goddamn it, Mike, if five hundred won't help, what's two grand gonna do? Kinda trouble you in?

mike

The worst kind, with the worst guy.

knish

KGB . . .

Mike nods his head.

knish

Didn't I tell you never let these guys get ahold of you?

mike

You told me a lot of things.

knish

Yeah, and you don't listen. I tell you to play within your means, you risk your whole bankroll. I tell you not to overextend yourself—to rebuild—you go into hock for more. I was giving you a living, Mike, showing you the playbook I put together off my own beats. That wasn't enough for you.

mike

Look, Knish, this time I don't need you to tell me how I fucked up. Every part of me hurts. . . . I know I fucked up. What I need this time is whatever money you can give me.

knish

See, that's the thing, this time there is no money. I give you two grand, what's that buy you? A day? No, I give it to you, I'm wasting it.

mike

That's fucking great.

knish

You did it to yourself. You had to put it all on the line for some Vegas pipe dream.

mike

Sure, Knish, I took some risks. You? You see all the fucking angles, but you never have the stones to play one—

knish

"Stones," you little punk? I'm not playing for the thrill a' fucking victory here. What am I, eighteen years old? I owe rent, alimony, child support. I play for money. My kids eat. I have stones enough not to chase cards, action, or fucking pipe dreams of winning the World Series on ESPN. Wasn't always that way for me. Back when I was twenty at Saint John's, I had my own dreams. I was third team All-America in *The Sporting News.* The captain the basketball team. Then I pop my knee, and the fucking coach comes in and cuts me. How's that for a bad beat? Just like that he loosed the dead weight.

Knish shakes his head at the memory.

mike

And now *you're* loosing the dead weight, huh?

knish

It's not like that, Mike. All the degenerates in this place, you're the one I can talk to. The only one I see myself in. You want me to call some people, try and get you some time, I will. Place to stay, or the truck, no problem. But about the money, I gotta do this. I gotta say no.

mike

Fine. I understand.

They begin to part, but Mike stops.

mike

Hey, Knish?

knish

What?

mike

I did put it all on the line. That's true. And you know what? It wasn't a bad beat. I wasn't *unlucky.* I was outplayed that time. But

I know I'm good enough to sit at that table. It's no pipe dream. I'm not chasing anything. I know all about obligations. I know about the scraping and the clawing . . . but I know there's more for *me* than just getting by.

Knish takes it in.

knish

I don't doubt your talent. . . .

mike

Listen, I never told anyone this. One night, seven, eight months ago, real late at the Taj, I see Johnny Chan walk in and sit three hundred–six hundred dollars. The room half stops and puts an eye on him, and he's just beating up the table. . . . Soon, after forty-five minutes, the craps tables are dead because all the high rollers are in watching, and some are playing with him. They're giving away their money so they can say they played with the two-time world champion. You know what I did?

knish

What?

mike

I sat down the table.

knish

No. You'd need fifty, sixty grand to play right in that game.

mike

Well, I had six. But I had to know.

knish

What happened?

mike

Played tight for an hour. Folded mostly. Then I made a score.

knish

Wired aces or kings?

mike

Rags. Chan raises. But I decide, just decide, that I'm gonna forget about the money, and fucking outplay him the hand 'cause I think he's got nothing. "Reraise."

                    knish
Reraise? You played right back at 'im, huh?

                    mike
And he comes right back over the top at me. Tryin' to bull me like all those fucking tourists he's been beating. I hesitate for like two seconds and again, "Reraise." Chan looks at me. Makes a move toward his checks, looks back at his cards, one more time at me . . . then he throws his hand into the muck. I took it down. "Y'have it?" he asks me. "Sorry John, I don't remember." I got up and walked straight to the cashier. I sat with the best in the world, Knish, and I won.

                    knish
You put a fucking move on Chan, you son of a bitch. . . . So that's why you made the run at that No-Limit game. . . .

                    mike
That's right. And I'll do it again if I can live long enough.

Knish nods as he absorbs what Mike says.

                    knish
Well, then I'm rooting for you, Mike.

                    mike
Yeah. . . . See you around, Knish.

Mike walks away.

int. petrovsky's office—night

Abe sits behind his desk, reading papers. He wears reading spectacles on the end of his nose. A single lamp illuminates the office. The sound of a knock, and Mike enters.

                    mike
Hello, Professor.

Abe pushes his spectacles up and peers at Mike.

petrovsky

Are you in pain, Michael?

mike

It's not that bad.

petrovsky

It looks fairly bad. Have you seen a doctor?

mike

No. No need. . . .

petrovsky

There's something else you need, perhaps?

Abe leans over and opens his desk drawer. There is the telltale clink of glass. He sits up with a bottle of gin and two mugs. He pours two drinks.

mike

Thanks.

Mike leaves his mug untouched.

petrovsky

Should I consider you withdrawn from school?

mike

I guess so.

petrovsky

Is this temporary? Will you be back next semester?

mike

I think we both know I'm no lawyer. . . .

Petrovsky drinks.

petrovsky

I hope my story didn't discourage you—

mike

No, it inspired me. I was already on my way.

petrovsky

But now you're here. Are you in trouble?

mike

Yeah, I am. Not with the law. I owe.

petrovsky

A gambling debt?

mike

Yeah, but not mine. I vouched for the wrong guy, and now it's on me.

petrovsky

You know, Michael, perhaps I can use my contacts, make it go away for you.

Mike thinks hard on this for a moment, as if he's calculating odds.

mike

I appreciate that, Professor, I really do. But living in this world, I can't do it like that.

petrovsky

I understand. So, what will it take for you to be free of this?

mike

I need fifteen thousand. Tonight.

Petrovsky breathes deeply.

petrovsky

So much? I'm not a wealthy man, Michael.

mike

I know. Kills me to ask. But it's the only play I have. Can you help me, Professor? Anything at all?

Petrovsky puts the top back on the gin bottle. He reflects and weighs.

petrovsky

I hate seeing your like this, Mike, and I want to help you. But fifteen thousand dollars . . . If it must be tonight, then ten is the best I can do.

mike

Will you do that for me?

Mike is tense. Abe finally nods.

petrovsky

When my mother let me leave the yeshiva it almost broke her, but she knew the life I had to lead. To do that for another is a *mitzvah*, and for that, I owe. So take the money and get yourself out of this trouble, Michael. I know you can.

Petrovsky locates a checkbook in the blizzard of papers on his desk. He writes out a check and hands it to Mike.

mike

I promise—

petrovsky

—Now listen, there's an all-night check-cashing place on forty-seventh and tenth, northeast corner. Speak to Moishe there, he'll cash my check, no questions. . . .

Mike gets up.

ext. checks cashed here—night

Mike walks up to the little box of a place and enters.

Through the plate glass window Mike is seen handing over his check to a fresh-faced young man, MOISHE.

Mike speaks, Moishe nods. He counts out money and hands it to Mike.

Mike exits, studies the money for a long moment, then tucks it into his pocket and moves on.

int. cage elevator—night

Mike stands in the coffinlike space of the elevator.

I've often seen these people, these squares, at the table. Short-stacked and long odds against, all their outs gone, one last card in the deck that can help them. I used to wonder how they could let themselves get into such bad shape, and how the hell they thought they could turn it around.

He pulls back the accordion door. The eye slat opens and Teddy's wide face fills it. The face chews.

The door is opened and Mike steps in.

int. kgb's card room—same

Teddy KGB, wearing colorful Coogi sweater the size of a carpet, smiles at Mike.

(v.o.) mike

Just standing here makes me queasy. The gray walls. The fucking mopes at the tables. The musty smell. I feel like Buckner walking back into Shea, but what choice do I have? . . .

teddy kgb

So you have my money?

mike

I owe you that money tomorrow, right?

teddy kgb

Da.

mike

So until then it's mine?

teddy kgb

Yes, for the next eight hours it's yours. But if you don't have it all by then, then *you* are mine.

Mike looks him in the eye.

mike

If it's like that, I have ten grand . . . and I'm looking for a game.

teddy kgb

What?

mike

You heard me.

teddy kgb

So you've learned nothing from that last shellacking I gave you.

mike

I've learned plenty.

Teddy commences thinking for a moment, and puts an Oreo in his mouth.

teddy kgb

So we'll play. Heads up. We both start with a coupla racks. Blinds twenty-five and fifty. We play till one of us has it all.

mike

Freeze-out, huh? Your game, your place—it's a sucker play.

Mike stares at KGB.

mike

Let's do it.

int. back card room—later

Mike and Teddy sit face to face across the card table. They each have eight thousand in hundred-dollar checks and two thousand in quarters in front of them. A few railbirds are around the table watching.

Blinds go in and Teddy deals them each two cards down.

ANGLE ON: Mike's cards. It's one of those things, he's actually got kings.

mike

Raise, Teddy. Thousand straight.

Teddy laughs.

teddy kgb

Very aggressive. "New day," and you won't be "pushed around."
But I reraise. Five thousand.

Teddy sits there, his mouth not moving.

(v.o.) mike

Doyle Brunson says the key to no-limit is to put a man to a
decision for all his chips. Teddy's just done it. He's representing
aces, the only hand better than my cowboys. I can't call, and give
him a chance to catch. I can only fold if I believe him, or . . .

Mike stares at Teddy while playing with his checks.

mike

Reraise. All in.

*Teddy gives Mike a withering case. He takes an Oreo out and unscrews it. He
considers the cream filling and . . . folds. He was trying to buy it.*

teddy kgb

Take it down.

He slides another deck to Mike. Mike rakes in the pot.

int. back card room—same

The board is out and some checks are in the middle.

(v.o.) mike

In a heads-up match the size of your stack is almost as important as the quality of your cards. I chopped one of his legs out in the first hand, now all I have to do is lean on him until he falls over.

mike

Tap. I bet your stack.

Mike puts in his bet.

teddy kgb

Call. I'll call.

Mike flips over his cards.

mike

Jacks up.

Teddy pushes his cards into the muck.

teddy kgb

They're good.

Teddy sits there. His rack is empty.

teddy kgb

Good hand. Catching that jack on the turn, you got lucky there. . . .

mike

Yeah, I'm lucky.

Mike starts stacking checks and putting them in their lucite racks. He has all four in front of him now.

teddy kgb

So that's it, then. Just like a young man, coming in here for a quickie. I feel so unsatisfied. . . .

mike

Real sorry.

teddy kgb

You must feel proud and good. Strong enough to beat the world.

mike

I feel fine.

teddy kgb

Me, too. I feel okay.

mike

Good. I'll just cash out, then. Pay ya and leave.

Mike stands up and puts on his jacket.

teddy kgb

'Course maybe we should check with one other guy, see how he feels.

mike

Who's that?

teddy kgb (calls out)

Grama.

Grama walks into the room.

mike

I thought I smelled him.

grama

I'll take what's ours.

Mike slides three racks to Grama.

teddy kgb

'Course you could let it ride, Mike. Take your chances. You'll let that happen, won't you Grama?

Grama shrugs.

grama

Sure, partner. He's still got till morning to make good.

mike

No thanks. I'll just keep the five left over.

teddy kgb

Fine. This is a fucking joke anyway. After all, I'm paying you with your money. . . .

mike

What'd you mean?

teddy kgb

Your money. I'm still up twenty grand from the last time I stuck it in you. . . .

Mike stops. A few railbirds comment in Russian and laugh out loud in English.

(v.o.) mike

They're trying to goad me. Trying to own me. But this isn't a gunfight. It's not about pride, or ego, it's only about money. I can leave now, even with Grama and KGB, and halfway to paying Petrovsky back. That's the safe play. . . . I told Worm, you can't lose what you don't put in the middle . . . but you can't win much, either.

Mike pulls the racks back toward himself.

mike

Deal 'em.

teddy kgb (yells)

Checks!

A Russian hurries in with new racks and sets them next to KGB.

mike

Double the blinds?

teddy kgb

Yeah. Table stakes.

mike

Feel free to reload at any time.

Teddy glares at Mike.

int. back card room—later still

ANGLE ON: Mike's stack. Fortunes have changed, and he's only got five grand left. Teddy's got towers. Empty racks litter the table. Grama paces menacingly.

The flop is out—A–C, 3–D, 5–S. The pot is a few grand.

ANGLE ON: Mike's cards—A–H, 5–D.

teddy kgb
You must be kicking yourself for not walking out when you could. Bad judgment, but don't you worry, son, it'll all be over soon. Bet's to you.

Mike puts his hand on his stack. He cuts out a huge chunk to bet with while Teddy puts an Oreo in his mouth and slowly chews. Mike stares at Teddy's mouth. Mike PAUSES.

ANGLE ON: Teddy's mouth as he slowly chews.

Mike removes his hand from his stack.

mike
I'm gonna check.

teddy kgb
No check here. I tap you.

Teddy pushes in a massive stack. Mike sits there staring at Teddy. Mike turns over his hole cards.

mike
I'm gonna lay these down. Big fucking cards. Top two. 'Cause I know you played two–four. And I'm not drawin' against a made hand.

Teddy tries to keep his face blank. He takes the pot, but he's startled, and some disappointment, or maybe even fear, peek through.

teddy kgb (to grama)
Lays down a monster. Shoulda paid me off on that. . . . (To Mike) The fuck did you lay that down?

Teddy stares at Mike. He looks at his stacks, he looks at his hands, he smoothes his clothes. He looks at his bag of Oreos and throws it across the room furiously. It explodes against the wall in a burst of chocolate crumbs.

mike

Not hungry, Teddy?

teddy kgb

Son of a bitch. Let's play some cards.

int. back card room—later

The room is now thick with cigarette smoke. The outer room's games have ceased and railbirds are leaning in heavily on the duel going on.

Mike has climbed back. He's got thirty grand in front of him, Teddy has about the same.

grama

Quit fuckin' around Teddy, finish it.

teddy kgb

Hangin' around, hangin' around. Kid's got alligator blood. Can't get rid of 'im.

Blinds are in. Two cards each go out, face down.

mike

Not going anywhere. Double the blind, two hundred.

teddy kgb

Fine, I call.

Teddy burns a card and deals the flop—6–D, 7–S, 10–H. It's Mike's turn to act.

mike

Check it.

Mike slams his hand on the table.

(v.o.) mike

Most guys would've gone on chewing slowly till they were dead broke. Teddy spots his own tell after one hand, he's that good. But no one's immune to getting a little rattled.

teddy kgb
Two grand.

Teddy flicks his bet in a bit too carelessly. Mike takes a moment.

mike
Call the two thousand, and don't splash the pot.

Mike bets his chips with care.

teddy kgb
You're on a draw, Mike? Go 'way, this one's no good for you. And in my club, I'll splash the pot whenever the fuck I please.

Teddy burns a card and deals a 2–C.

mike
Okay, okay. Still checking to the boss.

teddy kgb
That's right, Big Poppa bets the pot.

He pushes in the forty-four hundred in checks.

Mike looks at Teddy. He rubs his neck and cuts his checks with anguish. He slowly counts the same amount and puts it in.

mike
I gotta call, or I won't respect myself come morning.

Teddy burns a card.

teddy kgb
Respect's all you'll have left in the morning. Last card comin'.

Teddy deals the river—ace of spades.

Mike stares at the ace in pain. He seems tortured by that card, but trying to hide it.

mike (defeated)

Check.

teddy kgb

It hurts, doesn't it? You can't believe what fell. . . . All your dreams dashed. Hopes down the fucking drain. Your fate, standin' right behind me.

Teddy pushes in everything he has.

teddy kgb

That ace couldn't have helped *you*. I bet it all.

Mike hesitates, stands up.

mike

You're right, it didn't help me.

Mike pushes in all his checks, too. Teddy is dumbstruck as Mike flips his cards—8–S, 9–S.

mike

I flopped the nut straight.

Teddy flings his cards in and backhands the empty lucite racks off the table. A buzz of Russian goes up from the railbirds. The others groan in disbelief.

teddy kgb

Motherfucker. Motherfucker. That's it.

grama

That's it? The fuck do you mean that's it? Take 'im down, Teddy.

Teddy shakes his head.

teddy kgb

No more. Not this time. Son of a bitch checked it all the way. Trapped me.

Grama falls into a chair, looking beaten.

mike

Feeling satisfied now, Teddy? 'Cause I could go on busting you up all night.

The room grows tense. KGB, Grama, the heavyweight Russians bristle as Mike has clearly overstepped his bounds. . . . Then, Teddy shakes his head, and limply signals to one of his men.

teddy kgb

He beat me, straight up. Pay him. . . . pay the man his money.

Mike slumps forward toward all the checks as he realizes what he's done.

ext. park—day

Mike, a bag at his feet, stands across from the law school building drinking a cup of coffee from a cart. He has an unlit cigarette hanging from his mouth and it's been days since he changed his clothes. He looks exhausted, disheveled, but at peace.

Students filter by him, heading to school.

(v.o.) mike

Turned my ten grand into just over sixty. I paid Grama his fifteen, the Chesterfield got six, and after the ten going back to the professor, I'm back where I started—with three stacks of high society.

ext. law school building—same

Jo walks toward the law school building. On seeing her, Mike approaches her, the bag over his shoulder. She see him and stops as she reaches the steps.

jo

You look like hell.

mike

Should've seen me yesterday, Jo.

jo

Are you all right?

mike

Yeah, I'm okay. You?

She pauses, doesn't know where to start.

jo

I'm how I am.

She gestures to the bag.

jo

So you're outta here, huh?

Mike nods and pulls a thick, sealed envelope from his jacket.

mike

Nothing left for me here. . . . Listen, this has to go to Petrovsky.
He's still asleep, and I can't wait. Can I count on you?

jo

You could always count on me, Mike.

This hits him hard.

mike

Thanks.

*Mike turns to leave, then stops. He turns back around and pulls her to him.
They hold each other tight for a moment. Mike wipes a tear from her eye.*

mike

Take care, Jo.

jo

I'll try. And Mike, call me . . . if you ever need a lawyer.

mike

I will, and I will.

He kisses her once and goes. Jo watches him walk away.

                              jo

Hey.

Mike looks back over his shoulder.

                              jo

Premium hands.

He smiles.

ext. columbus avenue—same

Mike hails a cab and gets in.

int. cab—same

                    mike

To the airport.

                         cabbie

Where you headed?

                    mike

I'm going to Vegas.

Mike pulls the door shut and the cab begins to move.

                                        fade out.

the rounders glossary

a

all in—betting everything that you have in front of you.

alligator blood—a compliment given to an outstanding player who proves himself unflappable under great pressure.

apple, the—the biggest game in the house.

b

bankroll—the money a player uses to play poker with as opposed to the money he lives on.

base deal—cheating by dealing from the bottom of the deck.

belly buster—an inside straight draw.

berry patch—an extremely easy game.

blinds—a forced bet in Hold 'Em.

Brass Brazilians—the top hand, also known as "the nuts."

c

carpet joint—an upscale card room characterized by carpet on the floor. The opposite of a sawdust joint.

case money—emergency money.

checks—poker chips.

cowboys—kings.

d

down to the felt—totally out of money, broke.

e

eight ball—eight hundred dollars.

f

fast company—seasoned veterans who know what's going on in the gambling world. The opposite of Georges.

finger up your spine—a signal that you've been recognized as a cheater and had better leave.

Fifth Street—the fifth card dealt in a hand of stud poker.

fish—a poor player. A sucker.

flop—the first three community cards dealt in Hold 'Em.

Fourth Street—the fourth card dealt in a hand of stud poker.

g

George—a poor player. A rube.

give the office—to give a warning regarding cheating.

glimmer—money.

goulash joint—a restaurant or bar that runs a regular card game hidden in a back room.

Greek dealer—a player who cheats when dealing. A mechanic.

grinder—an unambitious player who only hopes to win a little money each day. Also known as a "leather ass."

h

hanger—a card that juts out conspicuously when a cheater is dealing.

high society—the highest denomination of chips in a card room.

Hold 'Em (also called **Texas Hold 'Em**)—a popular form of poker in which each player is dealt two cards facedown, called hole cards. The player may then use none, one, or both of his hole cards, in combination with five community cards dealt faceup, to make the best possible five-card hand.

l

ladies—queens.

live game—a game with lots of betting action. A "loose" game.

m

mechanic—a cheater who manipulates the cards to his benefit when dealing.

mechanic's grip—the way a cheater holds the deck to facilitate his manipulations.

mitt joint—a club where the house cheats the players, or one that turns a blind eye to cheating in general.

n

no-limit—a betting structure in poker that allows for the player to wager any amount he has in front of him.

nuts, the—the top hand.

nut straight—the highest possible straight in a given hand.

O

on the finger—money given on credit.

on tilt—an unbalanced emotional state that results in erratic play and the loss of money.

outs—live cards remaining in the deck that will improve one's hand.

p

Pasadena—fold.

play on your belly—to play straight up without cheating.

r

rabbits—weak players. Similar to Georges.

railbirds—spectators.

railroad bible—deck of cards.

rake—the percentage of a pot that the house keeps.

river—the final (seventh) card dealt in a poker hand.

road gang—a confederacy of cheaters.

rock garden—a game of extremely tight players.

rounder—a player who knows all the angles and earns his living at the poker table. The absolute opposite of a "sucker."

S

seconds—a style of cheating in which the dealer gives out the second card from the top of the deck, holding the top card for himself.

sign on your back—identified as a cheater.

slow rolling—an antagonistic way of revealing that you have the winning hand a little at a time.

soft—easy.

south—fold.

spikes—a pair of aces.

splash the pot—to throw, instead of place, ones chips while betting. This is frowned upon because it may obscure the amount of money actually wagered.

straighten out—to introduce an acquaintance to an underground poker club.

t

tap—to bet the amount of an opponent's entire stack, forcing him to go "all in" if he calls the bet.

tapioca—out of money.

tell—an unconscious gesture that reveals information about your hand.

tight—conservative.

turn—the second to last (sixth) card dealt in Hold 'Em.

w

white meat—profit.

Miramax Films

rounders

directed by
John Dahl

written by
David Levien & Brian Koppelman

produced by
Ted Demme & Joel Stillerman

executive producer
Kerry Orent

executive producers
Bob Weinstein
Harvey Weinstein
Bobby Cohen

Matt Damon

Edward Norton

John Turturro

Gretchen Mol

Famke Janssen

with John Malkovich

and Martin Landau

Michael Rispoli
Melina Kanakaredes
Josh Mostel
Lenny Clarke
Tom Aldredge

associate producers
Christopher Goode
Tracy Falco

director of photography
Jean Yves Escoffier

production designer
Rob Pearson

edited by
Scott Chestnut

costume designer

Terry Dresbach

music composed by

Christopher Young

music supervisors

*Amanda Scheer-Demme
Randall Poster

casting by

Avy Kaufman

A Film by John Dahl

A Spanky Pictures Productions

Mike McDermott	MATT DAMON
Worm	EDWARD NORTON
Jo	GRETCHEN MOL
Joey Knish	JOHN TURTURRO
Teddy KGB	JOHN MALKOVICH
Grama	MICHAEL RISPOLI
Dean Petrovsky	MARTIN LANDAU
Petra	FAMKE JANSSEN
Zagosh	JOSH MOSTEL
Savino	LENNY CLARKE
Judge Marinacci	TOM ALDREDGE
Barbara	MELINA KANAKAREDES
Griggs	MICHAEL RYAN SEGAL
Kelly	KERRY O'MALLEY
Birch	CHARLIE MATTHEWS
Higgins	CHRIS MESSINA
Steiny	HANK JACOBS
Wagner	KOHL SUDDUTH
Sherry	LISA GORLITSKY
Player	RYAN ANTHONY THOMAS
Roman	SLAVA SCHOOT
Maurice	GORAN VISNJIC
Bartender	JOHN GALLAGHER
Bear	MICHAEL ARKIN
Osborne	DAVID ZAYAS
Sean Frye	ADAM LEFEVRE
Vitter	PJ BROWN
Detweiler	MURPHY GUYER
Guard	GEORGE KMECK
Derald	BRIAN ANTHONY THOMAS
Roy	ERIK LARAY HARVEY
Henry Lin	PETER YOSHIDA
Kenny	RAY IANNICELLI

Irving	MAL Z. LAWRENCE
Sy	MERWYN GOLDSMITH
Freddy Face	JOE VEGA
Guberman	ALLAN HAVEY
Claude	NEAL HEMPHILL
Dealer	MICHELE ZANES
Cabbie	ALAN DAVIDSON
Sunshine	NICOLE BRIER
DA Shields	MICHAEL LOMBARD
Eisen	RICHARD MAWE
Judge Kaplan	BEESON CARROLL
Moogie	LENNY VENITO
Cronos	JOE ZALOOM
Taki	TONY HOTY
Zizzo	MARIO MENDOZA
Johnny Gold	SAL RICHARDS
Weitz	JOSH PAIS
Larossa	JOHN DiBENEDETTO
Churchill's Bartender	DAVID PHILLIPS
Judge McKinnon	VERNON JORDAN
Professor Green	MATTHEW YAVNE
Dowling	DOMINIC MARCUS
Property Guard	JOE PARISI
Tony	SONNY ZITO
Cocktail Waitress	NATASHIA PAVLOVICH
Jon Chan	HIMSELF

Stunts

Stunt Coordinator	JERY HEWITT
Russian Thug	JAY BOREA
Russian Thug #2	PAUL CICERO
Stunt Double Sy	JACK LOTZ
Stunt Trooper #1	PETER BUCOSSI
Stunt Trooper #2	NORMAN DOUGLASS
Unit Production Manager	CHRISTOPHER GOODE
First Assistant Director	CHRISTOPHER SWARTOUT
Second Assistant Director	PETER LETO
Production Supervisor	MARGO MEYERS
Post Production Supervisor	ROBERT HACKL
Poker Technical Consultant	MICHAEL SCELZA
Second Assistant Director	NINA JACK
Script Supervisor	LYNN LEWIS LOVETT
Art Director	RICK BUTLER
Assistant Art Director	HARRY DARROW
Set Decorator	BETH KUSHNICK, S.D.S.A.
Assistant Set Director	LORI JOHNSON
Leadman	CHRIS DeTITTA
Second	JOHN OATES, JR.

Set Dresser	GILBERT GERTSEN
	MITCH TOWSE
	DENNIS CAUSEY
	GORDON GERTSEN
	ROSS LATERRA
	JOE PROSCIA
	*TIM JOLIET
	*JUDY GURR
On-Set Dresser	BOB CURRIE
Master Scenic	JEFF GLAVE
Camera Scenics	PAUL DALE
	ROCHELLE EDELSON
Scenic Forman	KEVIN GOLDEN
Scenic Shop Person	RUTH ANN CECETKA
Scenic Artists	GARY JENNINGS
	JIM GEYER
	ELINA KOTLER
	ANNE SHERRILL
Property Master	RONALD C. STONE
2nd Props	STEVE GAMIELLO
Assistant Props	HEATHER KANE
	RICHARD DEVINE
Graphic Designer	LEO HOLDER
Art Department Coordinator	LARA KELLY
Art Department PA	TAMMY FEASTER
Camera Operators	MICHAEL GREEN
	LUKASZ JOGALLA
First Assistant Camera	STORN PETERSON
	JONAS STEDMAN
Second Assistant Camera	BART BLAISE
Camera Loader	MATTHEW FLANNERY
2nd Camera Loader	DARREN PERKELL
Steadicam Operators	JOHN CORSO
	JERRY HOLWAY
Steadicam Assistant	MARC HIRSCHFELD
Key Grip	GARY MARTONE
Best Boy Grip	PEDRO HERNANDEZ
Dolly Grip	RICH KEREKES
	DUSTY SMITH
Third Grip	MATTHEW CHUBET
	FRANZ YEICH
	JOSH STEINBERG
Gaffer	SCOTT RAMSEY
Best Boy Electric	MARK SCHWETNER
Third Electric	JOHN OATES
Genny Operators	MIKE MAURER
Assistant Costume Designer	EMILY LORETO
Wardrobe Supervisors	CHERYL KILBOURNE-KIMPTON
	ASKIA JACOB

Designer's Assistant	BEGA METZNER
Assistant Costumers	SANDI FIGEROA
	JILL ANDERSON
Additional Costumers	ALICE LEVY
	FIONNUALA LYNCH
Production Sound Mixer	MARK WEINGARTEN
Boom Operator	MARK GOODERMOTE
	ANDREW SCHMETTERLING
2nd Boom Operator	JOEL ARONOWITZ
Video Playback—24 Frame	BRIAN CARMICHAEL
Video Assist	EDWARD GLEASON
	DARREN RYAN
	IGOR SCUBSCIK
Key Hair Stylist	VICTOR DE NICOLA
Additional Hair Stylist	ANTHONY VEADER
Key Make-Up Artist	CARLA WHITE
Additional Make-Up Artist	RITA OGDEN
Special Effects	EDWARD DROHAN
Production Coordinator	ANDY ZOLOT
Assistant Production Coordinator	MERYL EMMERTON
Production Secretary	ANDREW VOGLIANO
Assistant to Mr. Orent/Mr. Goode	ROGER DAVIES (??PROD ASSOC)
Assistant to Mr. Dahl	SHERYL GIFFIS SWANN
Assistant to Mr. Damon	DREW CLARKE
Assistant to Mr. Norton	AMANDA KEY
Assistant to Mr. Stillerman	BARBRA DANNOV
Assistant to Mr. Demme	DONNA CINTORRINO
Office Production Assistants	CLIFTON FULLER
	PAMELA HIRSCH
Clearances	WENDY COHEN
Product Placement	TARA WALLS
DGA Trainee	ROGER LEE
Set PAs	JENNIFER DEMME
	GINGER GONZALEZ
	TED SHIELDS
	STAN WIENCKO
Production Accountant	KEN KROLL
Assistant Accountant	SUSAN STRINE
Payroll Accountant	JIM CARDEN
LA Casting Director	CAROL LEWIS
NY Casting Associate	JULIE LICHTER
Extras Casting	BYRON CRYSTAL
Location Managers	LYS HOPPER
	BILL BARVIN
Assistant Location Managers	MAURY WRAY
	JONATHAN ZEIDMAN
Locations Coordinator	JONATHAN SILVER
Locations Assistants	ROBERTO LOPEZ
	DEMIAN RESNICK

Unit PAs	SOL TRYON
	JASON FARRAR
	LUCY WALKER
Parking Coordinator	KO NIIZUMA
Unit Publicist	CARA LEIBOVITZ
Still Photographer	JOHN CLIFFORD
Craft Service	MIKE DUNN
Caterer	COAST TO COAST CATERING
Construction Coordinator	NICK MILLER
Construction Foreman	GORDON KRAUSE
Construction PA	GRETA ALEXANDER
Key Carpenter	LOUIS MILLER
Carpenter	JOHN FARRELL
Key Construction Grip	JONATHAN GRAHAM
Best Boy Construction Grip	MELVIN NOPED
Construction Electric	BOB BLAIR
Construction Electric Best Boy	TODD LICHTENSTEIN
Transportation Captain	LOU "SONNY" VOLPE
Transportation Co-Captains	RALPH VOLPE
Drivers	HERBERT ADE
	ROBERT ALBERGA
	FRANK APPEDU
	FRANK APICELLI
	PETER AQUINO
	CHARLIE BARRON
	RICHARD BATTISTA
	PETER CLORES
	MICHAEL EASTER
	GERALD GRIMES
	FRANCIS VOLPE
	BILLY FEATHERSTONE
	BOBBY FEATHERSTONE
	GEORGE HOLTZER
	EDDIE IACOBELLI, JR.
	TONY INGRASSELLINO
	TONY MARINO
	FRED MOMOLE
	REGIS MULLANEY
	WILLIAM McFADDEN
	JOHN RAFFONE
Animals Provided by:	ANIMAL ACTORS
Animal Wrangler	STEVE McAULIFF
First Assistant Editor	RICHARD J. ROSSI
Second Assistant Editor	STEPHEN M. RICKERT, JR.
Apprentice Editor	DARREN BLOCK
First Assistant Editor (NY)	JOHN COOK
Second Assistant Editor (NY)	JIM CRICCI
Apprentice Editor (NY)	ANDREW BUCKLAND
Post Accountant	LEAH HOLMES

*Sound Design	JON JOHNSON, M.P.S.E.
ADR Supervisor	VAL KUKLOWSKY
Dialogue Editors	ROBERT TROY
	BRUCE STUBBLEFIELD
Sound Editors	MICHAEL CHANDLER
	BEN WILKINS
	MIGUEL RIVERA
Assistant Sound Editors	CINDY JO HINKLEMAN
	CHRIS WINTER
Facilities Manager	GILLIAN JOHNSON
Sound Design by	FURY & GRACE DIGITAL
ADR Voice Casting	BURTON SHARP
Foley Artists	ZANE BRUCE
	JOE SIBELLO
ADR/Foley Mixer	JACKSON SCHWARTZ
ADR Mixer (NY)	BOBBY JOHANSON (SOUND ONE)
Re-Recording Mixers	JEFFREY PERKINS, C.A.S.
	CHRIS DAVID
Recordist	RYAN MURPHY
Post Production Sound	INTERNATIONAL RECORDING CORP.
Music Editor	TANYA NOEL HILL
*Additional Music Editor	THOMAS MILANO
*Temp Score/Music Editor	LORI ESCHLER FRYSTAK
*Music Consultant	RICKY FRYSTAK
Music Preparation by	JO ANN KANE MUSIC SERVICES
Orchestrations by	CHRISTOPHER YOUNG AND
	JONATHAN PRICE
Orchestra Conducted by	PETE ANTHONY
Scoring Coordinators	GERNOT WOLFGANG AND
	JONATHAN PRICE
Music Contractor	SANDY DeCRESCENT
Orchestra Recorded and Mixed by	ROBERT FERNANDEZ
Negative Cutter	GARY BURRITT
Color Timer	
Dailies by	TECHNICOLOR, NY
Dailies Advisor	JOE VIOLANTE
Camera and Dollies by	PANAVISION NEW YORK
Titles and Opticals by	HOWARD ANDERSON COMPANY
Color by	DELUXE
Insurance by	GREAT NORTHERN BROKERAGE CORP.
Legal Services by	DONNA BASCOM, ESQUIRE
Immigration Counsel	SHERMAN KAPLAN
	KAPLAN, KLEIN & ROGEN

the filmmakers wish to thank:
Billiard footage provided by
The Pro Billiards Tour, Spring Hill, Florida

Dog Racing footage courtesy of
The Palm Beach Kennel Club
Horserace footage at the Meadowlands courtesy of
The New Jersey Sports Authority
Major League Soccer footage provided by
Rogers & Cowan
Paintings by BUA courtesy of:
Bruce Teleky Inc. New York City
Photographs by Harold Roth courtesy of:
Sarah Morthland Gallery, New York City
Photographs by George Daniell courtesy of:
Sarah Morthland Gallery, New York City
Photographs by Henri Silberman courtesy of
Henri Silberman and Idealdecor USA, Inc.
Pictures of Dogs playing Poker by the artist Coolidge,
provided by The Archives of Brown & Bigelow, Inc.
World Poker Tournament Footage courtesy of
BINION'S HORSESHOE CASINO, Las Vegas, Nevada
Infomercial GLH courtesy of
Ronco Hair Products
Jim Albrecht of Binion's Horseshoe Casino
Mike Caro
Doyle Brunson
Jonny Chan
Diane Hanson of Leg Glamour Inc.
Genesis Publications
Paragon Publications
Mr. Slim Preston
Howard Schwartz of the Gambler's Book Club
Erik Seidel
Chuck Weinstock of ConJelCo Press
Mason Mamuth at Two & Two Publishing